D0777197

THE GUARDIAN

THE GUARDIAN

JOYCE SWEENEY

Henry Holt and Company

NEW YORK

Henry Holt and Company, LLC
Publishers since 1866
175 Fifth Avenue
New York, New York 10010
www.HenryHoltKids.com

Henry Holt® is a registered trademark of Henry Holt and Company, LLC.

Library of Congress Cataloging-in-Publication Data
Sweeney, Joyce.
The guardian / Joyce Sweeney.—1st ed.
p.   cm.
Summary: When thirteen-year-old Hunter, struggling to deal with a harsh, money-
grubbing foster mother, three challenging foster sisters, and a school bully, returns to his
childhood faith and prays to Saint Gabriel, he instantly becomes aware that he does, indeed,
have a guardian.
ISBN-13: 978-0-8050-8019-3
ISBN-10: 0-8050-8019-8
[1. Foster home care—Fiction.   2. Brothers and sisters—Fiction.   3. Schools—Fiction.
4. Bullies—Fiction.   5. Fathers and sons—Fiction.   6. Faith—Fiction.]   I. Title.
PZ7.S97427Gu 2009
[Fic]—dc22

2008040602

First Edition—2009
Printed in the United States of America on acid-free paper. ∞

10   9   8   7   6   5   4   3   2   1

To my editor, Kate Farrell,
who brings vision, creativity,
and joy to the process

THE GUARDIAN

Chapter 1

I start answering the door so I won't feel invisible. It's one of the tricks I've picked up in foster care—even people who hate you will cut you a little slack if you make yourself useful.

Andrea, in the corner, watches me make my move. I call Andrea The Watcher because whenever I think I'm alone, I'll get this cold feeling, like how you know there's a cockroach in the room, and there she'll be with her bulging forehead and bland blue eyes, recording like a machine in case I do something worth reporting to Stephanie, our foster mother. The grieving widow.

Andrea has done something weird to her hair today, like she confused the funeral with a prom. It makes her forehead jut out even more. She just started high school and she's already getting the message she's not exactly a magnet for boys. She's not actually ugly, but, as a guy, I can see why she doesn't get asked out. Andrea has no mystery. That sounds stupid, maybe, but I think it's true. You can't fall in love if there isn't some kind of mystery. Have you ever heard anyone say they love soft-boiled eggs? Andrea is like a soft-boiled egg.

I open the front door and two women storm in, almost stepping on me. I have to jump out of the way. I don't know them. I don't know most of the people here, filling up our living room, sitting on chair arms and coffee tables, filling our kitchen with sweaty casserole dishes. Most of them are women. Hey, who knows? Maybe Mike had something going on.

The two women push me out of the way and make a beeline to the couch where the Widow Stephanie is holding court in her new black dress from Saks, holding a black lace hankie up to her face, saying she doesn't know what she'll do now, four kids dependent on her, no emotional support, please make all checks out to cash, et cetera. I don't know what she's talking about. Mike was the kind of guy who would have a ton of insurance and since he was a veteran of the Iraq War, she's probably got a brand-new government check coming. But maybe she'll decide four kids are too many. I'll give you one guess which one of us she'd put in a sack and drown.

I decide to sit in the kitchen for a while, poking a fork into one of the casseroles. Room temperature mac and cheese clearly spiked with Cheez Whiz or some such chemical. But Rule Number One in this house is take nourishment whenever you find it. Just like it is with wild animals. You think ravens would eat carrion if they could go to McDonald's?

McDonald's is a Mike memory. Some Saturday mornings we'd do manly things together, like pull black leaf rot out of the gutters, and then we'd head out, just us, for a plastic tray of artery-cloggers. That's what Mike called the foods he loved. He made a big mistake, as it turns out, thinking that was a joke.

I listen to the high-pitched whine and chatter in the living room, longing to hear a deep voice. An image flashes in my head of Mike, lying on the ground, having his stroke, twitching like a hot wire. Cheez Whiz rises in my throat. I put the fork down and replace the aluminum foil cover like those sheets they put over the dead patient's head on TV.

I detect motion in the doorway. My eyes flick up. It's my foster sister Jessie. Jessie is The Stalker. I have a loving little pet name for each of my three sisters. Jessie is actually the best of the bunch. Her only flaw is that she's in love with me, not because I'm all that, but because I'm a guy who's thirteen and she's a girl who's twelve and we live in the same house without being related. Jessie is fighting forces beyond her control.

She stares at me now with her earnest freckled face, twisting her fingers into weird shapes in front of her skirt.

"Hunter? Are you okay?" One of Jessie's stalking techniques is to pretend to be concerned about me. It's effective too because that's something I'm sort of starving for.

But it doesn't work today. "Go away, Jess."

Of course, she doesn't buy that. She comes closer, slowly draws out a chair. "This must be harder on you than anyone else."

I wonder what she'd do if I grabbed her and kissed her. Enjoy herself probably. "I would think it's harder on Stephanie than anybody else," I say.

"But you . . ." Her clammy hand descends over mine. "You need a male role model." That's how she actually talks. Needless to say, she's the favorite of bullies all over our school.

I lower my eyebrows until I can hardly see. "Don't worry, Jess. I won't start trying on your dresses."

The clammy hand withdraws. A good stalker always knows when to retreat, so she can stalk another day. "I'll be in my room if you want to talk." She stands up, dark flowered dress swishing. I glance up to see her lifting her brown curls off her neck with one hand. For a second, she looks like a woman. It's creepy how girls our age keep morphing back and forth.

"Don't count on it," I mutter.

She swishes away, like she's sad for both of us.

I feel myself getting ready to replay Mike's stroke again, so I call up a different image. I think about The Motorcycle Man. If it can be said that anything good can happen when you're lowering a body into the ground, this would be it.

There we all were, this afternoon, trying not to hear the sound of the motorized coffin-lowering machine and Stephanie crying so loud it was like howling and suddenly: Vroom! Vroo-vroo-vroo-vroo-vroom!

We all looked up, automatically drawn to a better show. Some crazy man was riding his Honda through the cemetery.

Of course, Stephanie and her crew were horrified, hissing about respect and decency. Father Dunne took out his cell phone to call the cops.

But I was thrilled. My soul had almost been down in the grave with Mike after an hour of women crying and Father Dunne telling us that "the grass withers and the flower fades," and this guy with the big Adam's apple singing "You'll Never Walk Alone."

Suddenly, in the midst of that, something wonderful

had broken through and was now making a sharp, banking turn and coming to a stop about a hundred feet away from us.

And here's the best part—it seemed like the rider was looking straight at me.

I stared back. I memorized everything, from the Gold Wing logo on the bike to his helmet—black with a mirrored visor.

I forgot to breathe and gasped. Then the spell was broken and he stomped the gas pedal and roared away, scattering all the birds in the trees and throwing up a plume of dust that hung in the air, long after the roar of his engine had faded away.

"Outrageous!" said Father Dunne, before lamely trying to finish his act in front of a distracted audience.

I thought maybe it was some long-lost army buddy of Mike's, coming to pay his last respects.

So why did I keep feeling like the guy had come for me?

＊

"Hunter! What are you doing?"

I jump and drop the fork with a clatter. Thinking of The Motorcycle Man gave me an appetite and left me so deep in thought I had lost track of Stephanie. Usually I can follow her movements around the house by smelling the cigarette smoke.

"I was just . . ." I cough.

"Eating out of a casserole dish like the filthy pig you are, right? You're an animal!" She paces the kitchen, heels making a sound like artillery fire, her beautiful heavy dark hair swinging behind her as she pivots. My foster mother is pure evil, but she has gorgeous hair.

"My husband has died. Do you realize that, Hunter? Did it occur to you that instead of sitting here stuffing yourself and contaminating our food you could be helping me? Comforting me?"

She really isn't talking to me, so I don't answer.

She picks up a cake safe from the counter and shoves it into the crowded fridge, making something in there fall over with a clatter. "Maybe you could have been putting these dishes away for me, Hunter. Did you ever think about that?"

"I . . ." I pick up the mac and cheese to show my willingness to help.

"Just throw that in the garbage! You put a fork in your mouth and stuck it back in the dish! Do you think me and the girls want to eat your germs?"

I wonder about her friends in the living room hearing this. But they already know I'm her difficult child. I carry the dish toward the sink, careful not to get too close to her. Like a dog, Stephanie has an attack zone.

But I've misjudged. She lunges, grabs the dish from

me. "Just throw it in the garbage! Just throw it in the garbage like everything else!" She is shrieking. The casserole slips from her hands. The smell of Cheez Whiz fills the air. Glass shards go flying.

"Oh!" Her ruby-painted claws dig into my arm. "Look what you made me do!"

"I'll clean it up. You just go back out . . ."

She lets go and sits on the floor, dangerously close to the glass. She buries her face in her hands and sobs.

I feel bad for her. She's lost her husband. She gets overwhelmed with little stuff, so what is this doing to her? Cautiously, I put out my hand, hover it above her shoulder. "Stephanie. We'll be okay. . . ."

She shoves me so hard, my feet leave the ground. I land on my back, feel glass dig into my shirt. Macaroni squishes under my legs. I notice it's gotten very quiet in the living room, but no one comes to help. No one ever does.

Stephanie stands. She's a mess; raccoon eyes, hair disheveled. Her whole body is trembling. For a second, I think she might stomp me, but then she just turns and leaves the kitchen.

I lay still for a while, cuts and all. I've learned over the years the importance of resting up after things like that. After a while, I've got myself breathing normally.

I work calmly and slowly. It's good to have things to

do. I take off my shirt, pick the glass shards out, take the shirt into the laundry room, and put it in the laundry sink with a presoaker.

Then I pick up all the glass and throw it out, collect the macaroni pieces with paper towels, and clean the whole section of floor with a bucket and sponge. Pine-Sol and Cheez Whiz combine into a lethal smell. By then it's time to put my shirt in the wash. I put away all the casserole dishes, which takes some time, because there isn't much room in the fridge. I also put away all the candy, cookies, and pies. In the living room, I hear the first guests beginning to leave and I hurry up a little.

Using the back hallway, I go down to the bathroom we kids all share, strip, and take a long, hot shower. For insurance, I pour half a bottle of rubbing alcohol down my back, gritting my teeth at the burn, but knowing it's for my own good. There isn't much blood at this point. None of the cuts were really deep. It doesn't matter anyway. I can't put Band-Aids on myself.

I put on a T-shirt I can afford to ruin and jeans, and then I close the seat, sit down on the toilet, put my head in my hands, and cry so hard it feels like I'm trying to throw up.

The door opens. "I see your wee-wee!"

Sister Number Three, five-year-old Drew, aka The Screamer. This is a phase she's going through now, opening the bathroom door on me. I'm hoping it's a short phase. I also wonder what kind of sadistic builder put a pocket door on a bathroom.

She stares at me now with her angel face, her big brown eyes taking in the situation, realizing her mistake. "Hunter's crying!" she screams instead. She takes off down the hall, ponytail bouncing. "Hunter's crying! Hunter's crying!"

I decide to go to bed early.

Chapter 2

The next day is Monday and we're back to business as usual. Stephanie explained herself all day yesterday, saying she needed to go right back to work to "hold herself together." Personally, I'd like to take a day off from school and fall apart, but I know that's not going to happen.

I sit at the kitchen table, cutting a piece of toast into smaller and smaller squares with my knife and fork. Women and girls fly and flap around me in all their stages of dress and undress, and I feel like I'm looking at them from the end of a long tunnel.

"Drew, please eat something! You're going to make me late!" Stephanie is hopping on one foot, trying to pull the strap of a sandal over her heel.

Drew is using her spoon to draw circles in her oatmeal. "Can I have a banana?"

"I need five dollars," I say, trying to slip it in

through the confusion. "Our class is raising money to help the Red Cross."

"Five dollars! That sounds like an awful lot!" says Andrea.

"Who asked you?" I break into a light sweat.

"Well, if you're making a donation, the amount should be voluntary." Andrea has locked on me with her bland blue eyes. "I can't believe they'd tell you an amount you have to give."

God, how I hate her. I look at Stephanie, but she's not even listening. She's advancing on Drew with a hairbrush in her teeth.

"You can sit next to me on the bus if you want to, Hunter," Jessie ventures in a low voice.

I give her a vicious glare until she drops her eyes.

"How do you get your hair in such a mess just by sleeping?" Stephanie asks Drew, brushing furiously.

"I want a banaaaaaana!" Drew screams.

"Stephanie?" I try again. "Did you hear me? I need five dollars for school today."

"I'll loan it to you." Andrea smiles. "At twenty percent interest."

"I have five dollars." Jessie rummages in her bottomless backpack. "Mom, can I give Hunter the five dollars he needs?"

I look at Jessie across the table. I do want to be grateful, but . . .

"Don't give him money!" Andrea says to her. "He's always asking for money and making up stories about it. He's taking advantage of you!"

I wonder, since Stephanie isn't reacting to any of this, can she even hear us? She seems totally focused on brushing and ponytailing Drew. "Whose turn is it to make dinner?" she asks.

"Hunter's!" Andrea cries.

Actually, it's Stephanie's turn, but I'm not stepping in that. Anyway, the refrigerator is full of casserole dishes. "Yeah, it's mine," I say to Stephanie. "So anyway, could I please have . . ."

"Here!" Jessie thrusts a handful of crumpled ones across the table at me.

Andrea grabs it. "Stephanie! Are you going to let Hunter shake down his own sister that way?"

"Guys, please!" Stephanie says. "I can't hear myself think. Drew, let's go. I'm late!"

Drew starts to cry and hiccup. "I want a ba-na-na!"

Stephanie picks her up and carries her to the back door. We all pause and listen to the car rev up and head out. Then, like someone hit a button on a remote, we go back into action.

"Give me that money!" I lunge at Andrea across the table. She dangles it just out of my reach.

"Give it to Hunter!" Jessie whines. "It's my money and I gave it to Hunter!"

Andrea chuckles. "You hear that, Hunter? She talks like you're her ho."

"Shut up!" Jessie's fists are clenched and she's blushing furiously. She comes at Andrea, knocking her chair over, and they start going at it like a couple of WWE divas, only without the sex appeal. Like the heel I am, I snatch the money out of Andrea's hand and step over them on my way out.

Jessie and I wait side by side for the bus in uncomfortable silence. Andrea walks to Coral Springs High around the corner.

"Thanks," I finally say to Jessie, not making eye contact.

"You can't keep this up," she says softly.

"I know."

Luckily, the bus comes. I stand back to let Jessie get on first. Not because I'm a gentleman, but I want to see where she sits so I can sit somewhere else. Also, I'm in no hurry to see Duncan Presser. If I'm a ho, I guess Duncan Presser is my pimp.

He is sitting in the last seat on the bus, grinning at

me like a fat boy looks at a Thanksgiving turkey. Jessie sits near the front, looking at me hopefully. I move to the middle. It won't matter. Wherever I sit, Duncan will come to me. If I sit next to another kid, Duncan will just glare at them until they move.

I study my hands, while my peripheral vision monitors Duncan sliding in next to me. The seat groans.

"What kept you, man?" I say.

He guffaws. I amuse Duncan tremendously, but he's an easy audience. I can make him laugh by joking around, but also with easier things like blushing, shaking, crying, moaning in pain . . .

"Got my money, Girl-boy?" Duncan has a whole encyclopedia of pet names for me.

I silently pass him Jessie's five dollars, knowing that by making today easier for myself, I've made next week much harder.

"Hey, very good, Lambchop! I knew you were a smart kid." He snaps the money lovingly. "I'll bet that you're smart enough to come up with ten dollars by next Monday!"

Jessie turns in her seat and throws me an anxious look. I glare at her and she whips around.

"Duncan, it was really hard to get this. I can't . . ."

"Oh, yes you can! You can and you will. Just be creative, Cupcake. Sell drugs. Rob a liquor store. The important thing is to keep me happy. Remember the last time I wasn't happy?"

My right arm remembers every time it rains. "Duncan, you can't keep raising the price on me! If it was, even, like the same price every week . . ."

"I don't want excuses, Fruitpie!" He grabs my jaw, jacks it up so I have to look at him. "I want cash. You make it happen. Ten bucks next Monday. Or you die." He lets go and ruffles my hair. "Have a good week!" He lumbers back to his seat. All the kids who were staring quickly look away from me. I rotate my neck checking for injuries and finding none. I get a sneaky, sudden urge to cry but I fight it off. What choice do I have?

When I count up all the bullies in my life, it makes me feel bad, because I think there has to be something defective about me to make me such a target. I'm shorter than most of the guys (okay, and the girls) in my class, and thin, so maybe that's it. I just look easy to knock down. But Jessie, who is a bully-target, too, says we put out a vibe that whatever you give us, we'll take it, and whatever you take from us, we'll give it. I'd like to think maybe all foster kids are like that, but Andrea and Drew are normal, self-confident kids. My theory is that once you start feeling like a loser—and I started that pretty young—you can't stand up for yourself.

All this was to bring you to Mrs. Morales, my earth science teacher. She's the bully who disturbs me the most, because I know Stephanie and Duncan were born to be mean to people. But everyone likes Mrs. Morales. I like Mrs. Morales. But Mrs. Morales doesn't like me.

"Hunter, please take your seat," she says the minute my foot crosses the threshold. She doesn't say this to the other fifteen kids walking in. Do I look like I have a plan to not take my seat? To stand in the doorway and defy her?

I walk to a desk with my head down, already feeling bad before the bell even rings.

Did I also mention that Mrs. Morales is hot? She's about five-ten, most of it legs. She wears short tight skirts and real nylon stockings. Most of the female teachers have these sex-free uniforms: long denim skirt, long denim jumper, giant patchwork dress, like something the Taliban would come up with if they were into denim.

Mrs. Morales has shiny black high heels and her dress today is cherry red to match her lipstick. Jesus.

She paces in front of us, letting us settle in and mess with our books. "I assume all of you read your assignment last night." She looks right at me like I'm famous for not reading my assignments. "So can someone please tell me the difference between folding and faulting."

I know the right answer and raise my hand. She calls on someone else. She draws pictures of folding and faulting on the board while Sherry Studebaker pontificates. When she writes on the board, her skirt rides up on the right side and her whole body sways and jiggles. Jesus.

"Hunter?"

"What?"

She shakes her head. "Can you name an igneous rock besides granite?"

I am blushing so hard I can feel it. She always knows when my mind is blanking. I see she has written *igneous* on the board. When did that happen? I've lost time, like a UFO abductee, and the only igneous rock I can think of to save my life is granite.

"Can I name a sedimentary rock instead?" I can think of tons of sedimentary rocks. Sandstone, limestone, shale, conglomerate. The class laughs at my bargaining and she frowns, thinking I'm being disruptive on purpose.

"I need an igneous rock, Hunter. Did you read the chapter at all?"

"Yes, I read it!" I sound angry but I can't help myself. "You just happen to be asking me the one thing I don't know! Let me . . ."

"See me after class, please," she says and pivots away from me. "Anyone?"

Sinesha Williams says basalt. A rock I will never forget for the rest of my life. The igneous rock basalt.

I don't hear the rest of the class. I just stare into space, chanting in my head. Sandstone, limestone, shale, conglomerate.

After class she gives me a note to give to Stephanie. Of course I open it and read it. It says I am defiant. Stephanie uses that word to describe me too.

Jeez, what if I am? I'd think if I was defiant, bullies wouldn't be shaking me down for so much money.

"We're going to have to make some changes around here," Stephanie says at dinner, which none of us are eating because I heated up one of the casseroles and it's sort of gray and hard to identify. Sandstone, limestone, shale, conglomerate.

"What kind of changes?" Andrea asks.

Stephanie folds her hands on the table. "With Mike gone, things are going to have to be different. Everyone's got to help out more."

I look around the table at the person who has to do the dishes tonight, the person who has to take out the trash, and the one who cleaned the house after school today. None of them are Stephanie. What more are we supposed to do?

"Lots of foster parents don't honor their commitments." She pokes at the sedimentary casserole and puts down her fork. "Some of you already know that. You've lived in several homes. But I don't believe in that. The easy thing would be to say I can't handle the responsibility of four kids on my own."

I bite my tongue so I won't say that we're a source of income as well. Instead I say, "Didn't Mike have some kind of pension or death benefit or something?"

Everyone glares at me. I guess for using the word *death*. Or *benefit*. Or for putting the two together.

Stephanie aims a long red nail at me. "This is why all your teachers think you're defiant."

"Mrs. Morales isn't all my teachers!" I say, which just proves her point.

"It's great that you kids help with the housework," she goes on, now eating a slice of bread out of desperation. "But I'm going to need financial help from all of you as well."

I picture little Drew running a sweatshop sewing machine and think of *A Christmas Carol*. Are there no prisons? Are there no workhouses?

Andrea takes the ball. "We're underage," she says.

"Think outside the box," Stephanie says. This is

one of her favorite expressions along with *ramp up.* "There are lots of things kids your age can do. Mow lawns, babysit, bag groceries, get a paper route. We'll have a contest to see who can earn the most."

Drew bursts into tears. "I don't wanna get a job!"

"That's the best part, honey," Stephanie says. "I already thought of something wonderful for you. You're so cute and pretty. I was thinking we could get you into modeling, maybe even a beauty contest—you'll be a glamour girl!"

"Nooooo!" Drew wails. "Not a hammer girl!"

"You don't understand, honey," Stephanie says firmly. "It'll be fun, you'll see. And you might earn more money than your brother and sisters put together!"

I suppress another defiant comment about putting Drew out on the Internet and making some real money.

"I could . . . tutor," Jessie says. She's been very quiet up to now. "Or maybe give piano lessons to kids."

"Well, God knows I can babysit," says Andrea. "I've been doing it for free all my life."

Everyone turns to me, The Defiant One. Visions dance in my head. Getting up at three a.m. to pedal a bike through neighborhoods full of pit bulls. Putting boxes of tampons in Publix bags for the cheerleaders at our school. "Yard work," I say. "I love yard work."

"Great," Stephanie says. "Just make sure you get

ours done first. So the only real start-up expense we have is some head shots for Drew."

"Nooooooo!"

"Pictures, honey. Pretty pictures. It will be fun."

Drew pokes at her sedimentary dinner. "You always say everything will be fun," she mutters. "And then it isn't."

⁂

Some nights I can't sleep. This is one of them. It feels like too much is piling up on me. First, the single, horrible fact that Mike is dead. The loneliness and blackness of that fact, which my mind is just skirting around, for now. The thought of doing all our yard work without him and then having to use the rest of my weekends mowing other people's lawns. In addition to my house chores and my homework. The thought that Stephanie is my only parent now. The thought of Duncan Presser wanting more and more money every week while Stephanie is going to be paying closer attention to where all the money goes. Wondering why Mrs. Morales hates me. Andrea always watching me. Jessie stalking me, trying to get too close. A horrible picture of Drew dressed up in a French maid's outfit. Sandstone, limestone, shale, conglomerate.

That makes me think of Matthew, Mark, Luke,

John, bless the bed that I lay on. I wonder when was the last time I prayed.

I used to be religious when I was little. The first place I lived after my real mom gave me up was the Sisters of Charity. They had Saint Gabriel plastered everywhere because he was the patron saint of unwed mothers. There was a stained-glass window in the Sisters' chapel with his picture and I would look at it a lot, even though I knew the artist had made a mistake and given Gabriel blond hair. I know because I saw him the week before my mom gave me up.

The nuns thought I was great, being attached to an angel and praying all the time, but when I went to my second foster home—I was about six—I got a big brother, Toby. If I prayed out loud, he'd repeat everything I said in a high squeaky voice. If I prayed silently, he'd keep yelling, "What?" So I quit, just to get along. By the time I wound up with Stephanie and Mike, I had forgotten all about Saint Gabriel and my visitation. But I think about it now.

How he really looked, with his long jet black hair, like an Indian, with a halo of colored lights around his head. How he made promises to me, about staying with me and protecting me wherever I went. You might think this is a case of little kids imagining things, but it's a real memory. I'm sure of it. He came in through my bedroom window just like Peter Pan.

I guess I should have kept up those prayers, because he's definitely not watching over me now. I guess they don't like it much in Heaven, giving some slob kid a real visitation and then he falls off the wagon and forgets all about it. If I had any guts I would say a prayer right now and ask him to come back. But that would be so stupid.

The funny thing is, I dream about him. He's fused with The Motorcycle Man in my dream and he's riding his bike in slow, protective circles around the house. The sound of the engine is so real it wakes me up.

Chapter 3

I throw my weight against the lawnmower, sweat drenching the back of my T-shirt and dripping from my hair. I would take off my T-shirt, but the residents of Leisuretown don't like shirtless boys. Leisuretown is the cash cow I discovered this morning, a retirement development six blocks from my house. They all hire out their yard work, but they were sick of paying Mr. Schuster, who I hear about at every single house. Mr. Schuster charged too much. Mr. Schuster popped a sprinkler head and refused to replace it. Mr. Schuster swore at the cat. Everyone was ripe for my cut rates, sweet childlike face, and respect for cats and other animals. I picked up five clients, which is my limit for a given Saturday, and thought how proud Stephanie would be tonight when she saw how well I did. My biggest concern was that Mr. Schuster might show up and take out a contract on me, but that didn't happen. So I started this morning a happy, optimistic boy, working under the gentle sun, blackbirds singing in the trees and old people peeking fondly at me from behind their vertical blinds.

Now it's five o'clock in the afternoon and I'm only on house number four of five. The sun has turned evil and roasted me like a chili pepper and the blackbirds disappeared around ten this morning. No one has offered me lunch and only one lady gave me water, lukewarm in a plastic cup. If I wasn't taking sneaky drinks out of garden hoses, I'd be dead by now.

"Boy, are you finished yet?" Mrs. Collins calls from her doorway. "I want to start my supper."

I learned around noon not to ask questions, like, Why can't you eat supper while I'm still mowing the grass? "About five minutes, ma'am."

She closes the door without a word. I push harder and faster, but her "clipping bag" is full and I have to haul it to the backyard where she's collecting a pile of hay for some reason. Each house has had a hazard or obstacle of some kind. Mrs. Goldstein had an electric mower—I mean the thing actually plugged into a socket and had a cord that fell out about every twenty seconds. Miss Culp liked to come out and chat with me. I learned a lot about Harry Truman from her.

But here's the saving grace. Every one of them paid cash. As I trudge, I can feel the roll of bills that has been growing all day in my pocket. I feel good that I'm helping my family. The smell of cut grass has kept the memory of Mike with me and I almost feel protective of Stephanie, like I'm the man of the house now. I know that's corny, but it's making me see the whole point of the adult world. You kill yourself, but at the end of the day, you feel like a good guy. I mow the last square of Mrs. Collins's yard, empty the final grass clippings onto her haystack, wipe my face on my T-shirt, and ring the bell.

She opens the door. "I gave up and started cooking!" she scolds. "But let's see what you did."

She walks outside and inspects the whole lawn, glancing back at the house every few minutes, where her supper must be burning. I notice little shivers in the calves of my legs and wonder what she's cooking. I decide to distract myself.

"Why do you collect hay in the backyard?"

"It's a compost pile," she says. "I collect all the grass and leaves and put my garbage on top. It decomposes and makes a wonderful fertilizer. These days everyone throws away too much. I was raised on a farm in Iowa and we . . ."

Twenty minutes later—thank God for that supper on the stove—I've got my money and am free to go to my final job. As I leave Mrs. Collins's house, I see a vulture sitting on top of her compost pile. He probably thinks he's the luckiest vulture in the world to have found his own private landfill here in Leisuretown.

House Number Five is Mrs. Chang. She looks at my dripping, skeletal body in horror. "You look all tired out. Maybe you come back tomorrow."

I think how much I want to give the full amount to Stephanie and also how much I will need tomorrow off to collapse. "No, I'm good to go," I say. "I'm really thirsty, though. You wouldn't have anything like Gatorade, would you?"

"Who?"

"Maybe a glass of water?" I can smell her dinner cooking too. Rice, soy sauce, garlic. My knees buckle, but I manage to pull out of it.

"Okay, sure!" she says, and closes the door on me. None of these guys have let me in the house. Thank goodness when you sweat all the fluid out of your body you don't need to pee.

Mrs. Chang appears with a glass of V8. I'm not kidding. "No water?" I'm begging now.

"No."

I wonder what that could possibly mean. She must have a sink in there. I start to see what made Mr. Schuster so mean. But my tissues are screaming for fluid, even salty, blood-red fluid that tastes like beets.

"You be done by six," Mrs. Chang says. "Okay?"

"Okay." I stagger away. I see her cat lying on the driveway and remember to be nice to him. Actually, it might be two cats, since I'm seeing double off and on. "Good kitties," I say, just in case. I go to her garage to find the coup de grâce. A manual push mower. No motor, no gasoline. Not even a cord. I touch the bills in my pocket as if they were a rosary.

$\sim$

When I get home at six thirty, I don't smell any dinner cooking.

"Oh, Hunter! You stink! Go take a shower!" Stephanie greets me.

On my way through the living room to the kitchen, I try not to look at the thousands of photos of Drew spread out on the carpet, which Stephanie and Jessie are crawling around looking at. But I do catch a glimpse of both a pink feather boa and a cowboy hat. I fill and drink eight glasses of water standing at the sink, literally feeling my tissues swelling back to life. Then I go back for Round Two.

"I may stink," I say, dropping the wad of bills under Stephanie's nose, "but I'm rich!"

That gets her attention. "How much is this?" She scrambles for it like a kid at a piñata party.

"Eighty-two dollars. I mowed five lawns and got a couple of tips."

"Wow!" Jessie gazes up at me. She doesn't seem to care if I stink. "Andrea only made twenty-five dollars watching the kids across the street! I know I won't make anything like that tutoring."

Stephanie is busy counting. "Well, Jessie, that just shows you how early it starts. Men always make a disproportionate amount of money compared to women."

"You're very welcome," I say.

Money talks. "I'm sorry, Hunter. That wasn't fair," Stephanie says. "You worked very hard and this is just incredible. Can you make this much every Saturday?"

I can't remember her ever looking at me so kindly. Maybe I am the man of the house. "No problem," I say.

Andrea comes from the back of the house with her purse and her books, apparently headed to her second shift. "What happened to you?" she asks me. "You look like something ran you over!"

"Hunter made eighty-two dollars mowing lawns!" Jessie cries.

"Oh." Andrea actually seems to get smaller as she stands there. I totally understand. As the oldest, she wanted to make the most money.

"I heard you did a good job too," I offer.

"Yeah and . . . well . . . I'll get another twenty-five from the Bards tonight." She looks hopefully at Stephanie.

But Stephanie is looking at my eighty-two dollars.

Andrea shoves by me on her way out the door. "You stink."

"Hunter, after you shower you can help us look at these pictures of Drew," says my new best buddy Stephanie. "I decided to save money and go to Glamour Shots but I think they came out pretty good. I've already lined up a contest for her. *Good Homes* Magazine has a contest called Kindergarten Queens. The entry fee is only ten dollars, but if she wins, the first prize is five hundred. And we can use these pictures to start getting her into local pageants."

I try to skip over the concept that while Andrea and I worked hard all day, Stephanie and Drew were at the mall spending money. "Speaking of ten dollars," I say. "Since I did so good, can I have ten dollars? I need it for something in school next week."

This is the part where you're screaming at me right now, like the fans scream in the horror movie. You idiot. Don't go in the basement! Or in my case—you idiot. Why didn't you take the money off the top and never tell her about it?

It's only when I see that both Stephanie and Jessie have lowered their eyes that I realize what an idiot I was. I suddenly sway on my feet and feel dizzy. Drew's hundreds of little candy-box faces smile up at me.

"Well, Hunter," Stephanie says, casually putting the bills in the pocket of her pants. "There's really no point in making all this money if it doesn't go to household expenses."

I had to be the big man. I had to drop that whole wad in front of her so she'd see how big and bad I was. God, no wonder people take advantage of me.

"Stephanie," I say very quietly. "I worked really hard."

Jessie looks from me to Stephanie, obviously fearful of us both.

"Hunter, I'm sorry. Maybe when we get more on our feet."

I know this is crap. She's getting Mike's life insurance and support checks for all of us and she works in real estate, for God's sake. I know that she probably had a nice lunch at the mall with Drew and bought her who knows what kinds of clothes and stuff for her new career. I know she's screwing me over and there's nothing I can do.

"I'm gonna take a shower," I say.

"Okay." Stephanie keeps her eyes down. It's good to see she has some small sense of shame.

Jessie jumps to her feet. "I'll bet you're hungry. I'll make you a sandwich."

I feel dangerously close to tears. "That would be really nice, Jess."

I pass the family room where Drew is watching *SpongeBob SquarePants*. "Was it fun being like a supermodel?" I ask her.

She doesn't even turn around. "Yuck!"

"I don't like my job either."

I take a long, long hot shower, tipping my head back to drink even more water. I turn the water up to the hottest setting and let it pound on my sore shoulders. As the sweat and dirt go down the drain, it feels like that's my day going with it. It was really all for nothing.

In my room, I find the final insult of the day. Somewhere between her jobs, Andrea has explored my room. She does this on a regular basis, not because I have anything interesting, but just because she can't help herself. She needs to become a detective when she grows up. She tries to be careful, but I see a desk drawer that isn't pushed all the way in, the bed is made differently than the way I made it, and for some crazy reason, one of my pictures, the framed photo of my favorite wrestler, Rolan Thunder, is hanging crooked. I guess she wanted to see if I had put in a wall safe and filled it with jewels. I straighten everything back up—if you've ever lived in an institution you develop this habit of keeping everything in perfect order—and pull a clean T-shirt over my head. I can tell from the smells drifting in from the kitchen that Jessie didn't make me a sandwich, she's cooking a meal for me. She's really the nicest person in our house. I don't know why she gets on my nerves.

It's Sunday night and I can't sleep. Partly because I slept all day. Stephanie and the girls all went to Mass and then probably out for pancakes with more of my money, but no one minded that I wanted to stay in bed all day. It was a combination of exhaustion and depression, but now, when I should be sleeping, I'm all wired. I can't find a comfortable position. It feels like mosquitoes are buzzing in my head. I want my money.

I worked my ass off all day Saturday and Duncan Presser is still going to beat me up tomorrow. Since he's done it three times before, I know it will come at lunchtime. On the morning bus, he'll just act disappointed and sad, taunting me with phrases like, "What are we going to do about this, Goldilocks?" But he knows enough not to make any major moves in front of the driver. All during the morning, every passing period he'll find me in the hall and say, "How you doing, Sweetheart? See you at lunch."

He's smart. Lunch is the easiest time to catch somebody alone and pull them into a vacant classroom. I've tried hiding, but he always tracks me down. I have no friends, so it's easy to get me alone. Either on my way in to lunch or on my way out, he'll appear by my side and

steer me quietly to his room of choice, close the door—
bam, bam, bam—really fast and leave. He's good.

In case you're wondering, I tried the route of telling a teacher what was happening, but Mr. Seeger told me that this was the kind of thing I should work out for myself. I felt like he was telling me I was a sissy if I didn't fight back against this kid who outweighs me by fifty pounds. Maybe I should have told a female teacher. Maybe I'll try that tomorrow.

No. I shouldn't have to do any of this. I earned eighty-two dollars on Saturday and ten of it should be mine, by all that's holy. I find myself standing up in the dark, standing beside my bed like my legs have taken over. I'm going to go get my money.

My heart goes into hyperdrive at this thought, but it's a good kind of excitement—like at the end of an action movie when the final big fight scene starts. I feel powerful that my legs are taking the initiative. I move slowly, like a stalking animal, getting my bearings in the dark.

I pass Andrea and Jessie's room and see a slice of light coming from under the door. I wonder which one of them is up so late. I don't know the time, but it has to be after one o'clock. I take my steps slowly and carefully so I won't squeak any floorboards. I pass Drew's room, where the door is slightly open and I can hear her snoring. I keep feeding my anger with thoughts so I don't chicken out. Stephanie is exploiting all of us, using us, robbing us. Somebody has to strike back.

Stephanie also sleeps with the door open, so she can hear if Drew needs anything. We used to joke that she and Mike closed the door only when . . . you know. I guess now it'll be open forever. My heart is hammering away, but I feel strong and steady, almost like you feel in a dream where you face the monster and it crumples in front of you.

Inside the doorway, though, I sort of freeze. I see Stephanie in bed and feel guilty, like I'm doing something dirty coming in here. She's half-lit by her big digital alarm clock, which tells me it's 2:15. She's wearing a man's shirt that must be Mike's and I quickly turn away because that little detail could melt me and destroy my mission.

Stephanie keeps her purse on the shelf in her closet. This part is tricky because it's a darker part of the room and there's a turn and a half wall, so I put my hands out in front of me and go very slowly. In my usual way of not thinking things through, I suddenly realize that I won't be able to figure out what's a ten-dollar bill in the dark. I stop for a minute, all systems short-circuiting, and consider an abort.

No. I never stand up for myself. I always run away. If I stand here and think, I'll figure this out. Maybe I can close her closet door and turn on the light. No, that's way too risky.

Then I picture it. Since Stephanie runs around in her car all day, she's loaded down with security devices and one of them is a little flashlight on her key chain that you squeeze. This is so you can find the keyhole fast and get into the house or the car before the bad guy catches you. I can use that tiny little light to look at the bills. My legs get brave again and I move forward.

Their closet—her closet—is a walk-in. As soon as I round that wall, I feel safer because even if she half woke up, she wouldn't see me. I see the dark mass on the shelf that is her bag. It's as big as a piece of carry-on luggage and I lift it down carefully with both hands, so it won't clunk me on the head.

The closet smells like Mike's aftershave. I try not to think about that.

I sit on the floor, so there's no chance of dropping the purse. Struggling to breathe slowly and calmly as I rummage around, trying to find that key chain . . .

A siren blasts out, louder than a police car on a high-speed chase. Stephanie must have bought one of those purse alarms. All circuits freeze, chemicals flood my body. Stupid, scared chemicals that keep me from running for my life, like I should.

After that, there is no real time sequence. Just a

bunch of images that come to me only later. Lights springing on. Stephanie rounding the closet doorway like she's blown by a huge wind. Her screaming at me. My back hitting the wall. My sisters in the closet doorway screaming at Stephanie to stop hitting me. Me, alone on the closet floor, curled up and panting.

I don't know how I get back to my bed, but somehow I'm there and the house is dark and quiet again. Except for a lot of pain, it's like the whole thing was a dream. Only now I know that Stephanie will always see me as a thief and watch my money like a hawk. And tomorrow, Duncan Presser will beat me up all over again.

I feel myself sort of cracking up, like splitting into two parts. One part of me—no, it's all of me—slides out of bed and lands on my knees. I fold my hands on top of the sheet. I'm six years old, back with the nuns. Words come out of my mouth.

"Gabriel, please. Come back to me. I know I forgot all about you, but I need you now. I can't do it on my own. I know it's bad to come to you just because I need something, but please help me. All I need is ten dollars before lunch tomorrow. That's all. I don't want to get beat up again. I can't take it. I'll go crazy if one more person beats on me. Please. I wasn't stealing. She was stealing from me. I know I don't go to Mass, but I'm a good kid. I swear I've been a good kid all this time and now Mike is dead and I don't have anyone to help me but you. I know you're real. You used to come to me and you were real. I believe in you. I believe in you. Please."

After that, it mercifully deteriorates into crying. I haul myself back into bed, totally ashamed and really glad no one had been around to hear that. We all go crazy in different ways, I guess. Being religious is better than getting a handgun and shooting up the family, right?

Of course, neither one solves the problem. But at least I'm so worn out, I can sleep.

Chapter 4

The distant growl of a motorcycle engine wakes me up and I wonder if I'm going crazy. That's something I actually worry about a lot. Dr. Phil did this whole show on what kind of kids are prone to turn out bad and it was my biography.

Any guy who is disconnected from his father is something like ten times likelier to end up in prison and if you put disconnected from his mother into the equation, you might as well throw me in the trash can right now. And my chances of going insane are really high too. So I've always watched myself carefully for the signs.

But now, when I hear that motorcycle engine at five a.m., I jump out of bed and run to the window like I think Santa is coming.

And I see him.

Clear at the end of my street, turning the corner. I know it's the same bike I saw at the cemetery. I see the angel-wing logo and the mirrored visor. And then he's gone and I stand there wondering if I really saw it at all.

⌖

Jessie and I walk to the bus stop in silence. My sisters are always quiet and respectful of me after Stephanie has beaten the crap out of me. Jessie, in particular, probably thinks I'll bite her head off if she asks how I'm feeling, but today I feel different.

"Thank you for making dinner for me on Saturday," I say. I keep my head down as her head swivels toward me in astonishment.

"You had to be hungry after mowing all those lawns," she says. Then she adds quietly, "Stephanie should have given you some of the money. I wish I had some so that . . ."

"Why don't we sit together on the bus?" I say, pretending to study the Skylark Pest Control van parked across the street. "I know he's gonna get me sometime today, but if I sit with you, he might not taunt me about it this morning."

Her gaze scorches my face. "Of course I will, Hunter. Of course I will. Anytime, all you have to—"

"I want to ask you a question, Jess. A serious question. A deadly serious question."

I finally meet her eyes and see that her expression is

just a little worried. I'm sure she's reviewing what she knows about snipers and bombers too. "Sure."

"At Mike's funeral, there was a guy on a motorcycle who rode through the cemetery, right?"

She frowns. "Yes. He screwed up the whole service."

"He drove all around the graves and stopped in front of us and he had the Gold Wing logo on the bike, right?"

"Right. Why are you asking me?"

I don't answer, just nod to myself. I'm not hallucinating. That's a good thing.

When we get on the bus, Jessie actually looks reluctant to sit with me but a promise, with her, is a promise. And the trick actually works. Duncan smiles at me but he stays in his place. At least for now.

Here's a miracle: When I get to my locker this morning, there's a girl waiting to talk to me. It's Carolina (nothing finer) Cummings, who wears soft sweaters (butterscotch today) and has long black curls. She's in Gifted just like me, but the other girls shun her because she's too sexy. This is one reason I'm glad I'm a guy. If a guy is an outcast, he gets ignored or beat up. But girl-society has all these cruel little whispery, giggly, note-passing things they do. And what did Carolina ever do that was so bad? She got boobs before the rest of them.

"Hi, Hunter," she purrs. She's holding her books up over the goods today.

"Hi," says witty, clever me. Then, unable to look at her anymore, I turn and fumble with my lock, which I no longer know the combination to.

"We have to pick a partner for our science project," she says. "You want to do it with me?"

I wrestle with my lock, sweating. Her question echoes in my head like the loudspeaker at a truck rally. I ask myself crazy questions—Does she like me? Am I cute? But when I get back down to Earth, I realize I'm the only one she can ask. In our gifted science class, there are only four guys and the other three are even lamer than me. And no girl would partner with her.

"Sure," I say, finally jerking the lock open. There's some kind of white envelope on the bottom of my locker that somebody must have slid through the grate. Maybe I am cute.

"Cool," says Carolina. "You want to eat lunch with me today and we'll talk it over?"

I get distracted, looking at the envelope, which has my first name written in spidery pencil—I don't recognize the handwriting at all. I hope I'm not in trouble.

"Uh—sure." Maybe Duncan won't beat me up today at all. Maybe Carolina will blind him with her beauty and I can sucker punch him.

"Okay," she says, frowning at the letter like it's making her jealous. "I'll meet you in the hall outside the cafeteria." She gathers up her hair and tosses it behind her shoulders, pivots like a runway model, and sashays—there's no other word for it—away. I try to keep my tongue from hanging out.

When all the blood returns to my brain, I open the envelope. A ten-dollar bill falls out. I look at the envelope to see if it's from Jessie, disguising her handwriting, but I don't think so. When she does stuff for me she wants full credit.

My knees go funny for a second and I lean against the locker door, pushing it shut. I think of The Motorcycle Man. I think of my silly prayer last night: Give me just ten dollars before lunch tomorrow. I stare at the envelope again, wondering what an angel's handwriting would look like.

The lunch menu for today at Sawgrass Middle is a fish hoagie, spaghetti, salad bar, peas, canned pears, and a ranger cookie. If you're familiar with "elementary and secondary" school lunches, you'll know the only safe choice above is the canned pears, because they don't do anything to them and leaving them out for hours won't hurt them, like it does the salad bar ingredients. I don't think I need to explain why fish is a problem, the spaghetti sauce is always orange instead of red, the peas have been nuked until they have no texture or food value, and although the ranger cookie usually tastes good, a lot of kids think they slip something in it to keep us calm. So today, I'll be eating several dishes of pears.

I don't usually pay attention to morning announcements and what the lunch is going to be, because my usual lunch plan involves buying a bag of chips from the vending machines and eating them in a deserted classroom. Then, if it's a big social day for me, I'll head over to the media center. The media center is like the homeless shelter of middle school. They'll always take you in.

But I'm a different person today, walking through the halls with Carolina, whose curls, and everything else, bounce when she walks and whose eyes sparkle when she talks. Her conversation is pure nerd. She is actually excited about doing a project on sediment, but she's so beautiful, I don't care.

"I was thinking, like, we could mix up different things, you know? Sand, mud, something else, maybe something shiny so it would look really good, you know? And let it settle and it would make layers, you know? Do you think it would? I mean, why wouldn't it? Because that's what it does in nature."

My contribution is to insert, "Yeah! Yeah! Yeah!" like I'm sure Monsieur Curie did to encourage Madame

Curie when she was on a roll. Then I bump into something. Something big.

It's Duncan.

At first, he's got his bully grimace on because he can't even wrap his mind around the idea that Carolina is with me. He must have figured we were like two pieces of flotsam, caught in the student stream, but not really together. But when I stop short, she stops with me and Duncan just stares, the slow chip in his computer struggling to figure this out.

I have the ten ready in my shirt pocket, but I don't reach for it just yet.

"Do you want something?" Carolina asks Duncan.

"Uh . . ." His eyes fix on her chest. He is incapacitated.

"We're in a hurry," I say. I take her hand, which is made out of silk and cream, and pull her around him and on to freedom.

"Are you actually friends with him?" she asks me as we leave him in our wake.

"You know what would be really cool?" I say. "Some tiny little seashells. Or, I know, that glitter powder. That would look like mica."

"Oh!" She squeals. "That would be so cool!"

"Get anything you want for lunch," I tell her. "I'm buying."

Carolina chooses the orange spaghetti, so I do too. It's time for me to start living on the edge. As we leave the line, I see people staring at us. For the first time in my life, I like being looked at. I know they're thinking, What did he do to get her? I feel like I'm actually taller with every step I take.

One little downer. In that sea of faces, I pick out Jessie, sitting all alone at the end of a table. Usually she has a couple of loser girlfriends hanging around and I wonder if she banished them for today, hoping the bus ride meant we were starting up a romance or something. That's how girls think, I'm not kidding. I feel almost angry looking at her. Doesn't she know she's a little seventh grader? What does she expect?

"Where do you want to sit?" Carolina asks. When she stands still, she sways a little, like a palm in a light wind.

"Over there." I point to the opposite end of the cafeteria, away from Jessie's stalker eyes. I'm having the best day of my life. I'm not gonna mess it up by feeling guilty.

When I get home that afternoon, everybody is in the kitchen. It's Jessie's turn to cook and she's standing at the stove, giving me the fisheye.

"What's for dinner?" I ask.

She gives me a nasty smile. "Spaghetti."

Well, at least it won't be orange. Jessie is a great cook, the best we've got, and she makes everything from scratch, which is why she's working on a sauce at four p.m. No Ragu for her.

Stephanie, Andrea, and Drew are all sitting at the kitchen table, making up cute answers for the Kindergarten Queens magazine contest. Drew rolls her big eyes at me like a hostage trying to signal the FBI.

"Hobbies. What should her hobbies be?" Stephanie asks Andrea.

"Something physical, something mental, and something spiritual," Andrea suggests.

I pull up a chair. "How about snowboarding, chemical engineering, and Buddhism?"

Now Stephanie gives *me* the fisheye. "If you're not going to be serious, at least don't distract us."

"I don't want boob-ism!" Drew begs.

Jessie, at the stove, snorts. "That's *Hunter*'s new hobby."

Andrea looks up at that and files it in her snoopy brain. I need to create a diversion. "Why don't you do something crazy and list her real hobbies?" I say. "Eating paste and pulling the heads off Barbies."

Drew laughs happily. "Put that down!" she says to Stephanie.

"No, honey, that's macabre." She turns back to

Andrea. "How about collecting Barbies, though? That sounds upscale."

Andrea tilts her head. "Collecting multicultural Barbies!" she offers.

"Oh, please!" Jessie and I say in unison, while Stephanie writes greedily.

"What is that?" Drew tugs on Stephanie's arm.

"Is this how you made out your résumé?" I ask Stephanie, planting my feet carefully in case I need to jump out of range.

But I'm being ignored as much as Drew. "I think she should cook or bake things," Andrea says. "Put down, trying out new cookie recipes."

"I gotta go," I say. No one rushes to stop me. Drew's eyes follow me to the doorway, then swing back to Stephanie. "Can I go too?" she asks.

"Don't you want to hear what we're writing about you, sweetheart?"

"No!"

"Well, okay. Run along."

Drew follows me down the hall like a little penguin. "Can I help you with something?" I ask her. She follows me into my room and sits on my desk chair while I flop onto the bed.

"Hunter, I don't want to be the queen. I don't like taking pictures of me and making up lies. Stephanie says someday I have to stand in front of men in my bathing suit. I don't like it."

"You can't take it seriously, Drew. It's just a game. It's not real. You dress up and you play the game and then you either win or lose and you can come home and relax."

She is shaking her head emphatically. "No. It's not a game. It's real. Stephanie is trying to change me into a doll."

Usually I think of Drew as a minor annoyance, like radio static or mosquito bites, but when she says this, it's as if she reached into my chest and grabbed my heart.

"Is that how it feels to you?" I almost whisper.

Her voice rises to a low wail. "What if I change into a doll and I can't change back?"

I think of Carolina and some of the other girls in school. I realize Drew is not just a little kid seeing a monster under the bed. She's talking about something important, whether she understands it or not.

I lean forward. "Drew, I totally agree with you. I think this is a real stupid thing to do to a little girl. But you just have to remember she can't change you into anything."

"You have to stop her, Hunter."

"Me? What do you think I can do about it? Stephanie's on the trail of money. You might as well ask me to step in front of a moving train."

"When she puts that letter to the magazine in the mailbox, you steal it and tear it up into a million pieces. Then I won't be the queen and maybe she'll give up."

I have the stupidest urge to cry. "I can't steal out of a mailbox, Drew. They'll put me in jail if I do."

"Do it at night and they won't see you!" She's breathing hard, desperate. When you're five, I guess you think a thirteen-year-old boy can do anything.

"No, Drew. They guard the mailboxes. They have locks on them. There's no way I can do that for you. I would if I could."

She stares at me. "Okay, Hunter." She slides off the chair.

"Maybe I can talk to Stephanie. Maybe I can do something."

She's trudging out, looking at the carpet. "Yeah, maybe."

She closes the door. I hold my breath so I won't cry. I wonder how hard it would actually be to break into a mailbox. I want so much to be what Drew thinks I am. A magical savior.

A guardian angel.

Someone gave me that ten dollars.

I get on my knees. Rolan Thunder looks down from his poster like he thinks I've lost my mind. But what have I got to lose?

"Saint Gabriel?" I try not to listen to my weak little voice. "Thank you so much for the ten dollars. And thank you for sending Carolina to me and making Duncan leave me alone. You solved, like, half my problems in one day. I mean, I think I might get an A on the science project and then Mrs. Morales might like me better too. I mean, it's really cool how you worked everything out for me and if I end up being . . . friends with Carolina . . . well, that's maybe too much to ask for but anyway . . . I want something that's not for myself. I'm not testing you or anything, but Drew really doesn't want to be in that contest. Can you stop the envelope from getting to the magazine? I mean with the other stuff you did today, I would think holding up one little envelope wouldn't be a problem. Not that I'm questioning you. It would mean a lot to me. She's a good little kid, and I don't like what Stephanie is doing to her. Please help me and thank you in advance if you do. I'll pray to you every day if you do this thing for me. Thank you. Amen."

I stand up, brushing off my knees, feeling like a fool. But hopeful.

Chapter 5

In the media center, I find a book called *A Dictionary of Angels, Including the Fallen Angels.* Now how in the world, I wonder, did that book get into a school library? The left-wing guys should have nabbed it for promoting religion in a public school. The right-wing guys would definitely not want us reading about fallen angels. But I'm used to miracles by now, so it doesn't really surprise me that this book is here for me to find.

I learn that angels, in the whole history of people interacting with them, are more complicated than I thought. Apparently, the Zoroastrians got the first glimpse of them and passed the idea to the Hebrews, who passed it to the Christians, Muslims, and so on. But during all those thousands of years, it's not a consistent team of good guys on a mission. Some of the angels (not fallen) hang out in Hell, exchange jobs, and even names, with other angels, piss off God, get suspensions, even come down to Earth and get into fistfights with humans. Pretty cool. There are girl angels, leopard-spotted angels, shape-shifting angels, you name it. And that's without getting into the fallen angels, which I skip over because I don't want to think about stuff like that. It's scary enough to have a good-natured spirit coming after you. But from this overview I can see that finding a guardian angel in black leather riding a motorcycle is perfectly within the realm of angel norms.

Next I go to the section on Gabriel. I know I'm counting on a memory from age four, but I can still remember that when I had my Visitation, he asked me, "Do you know who I am?" And I said, "No." And he said, "I'm Gabriel. Hasn't your mom told you anything about me?" And I said yes, and he seemed to like that. Another thing I remember is that when he came through my window, he said, "Hunter, don't be scared." He not only knew my name, but he used the standard angel greeting. Check your Bible. Every time they appear to someone, they say, right off, "Be not afraid." And with good reason.

I learn that my guardian angel is one of the top guys in the organization, running second only to Michael. Saint Gabriel is the angel of annunciation, resurrection, mercy, vengeance, death, and revelation. He is the Prince of Justice and the Angel of War. According to the

Babylonians, he fell into disgrace once for not following one of God's commandments to the letter, but he was reinstated after a while. So I guess he is some kind of rebel. He was the angel who helped Joan of Arc and he also appeared to some pastor in Indiana, where he left his footprint in some wet cement. Of course his biggest claim to fame is his big scene with the Mother of God, which is what makes him the protector of illegitimate children. Like me.

As I'm reading along, I start to smell flowers. If you were raised Catholic, you know this is something to pay attention to, since Mary and some other saints are supposed to scent the air with roses when they appear to you. So my spine starts to prickle. Then I feel two hands on my shoulders and I scream.

Everyone in the media center, especially Mrs. Wolfe, the media director, stares at me.

"Hunter! Did I scare you?" It's Carolina Cummings, sliding into the chair next to me as I blush and scramble to hide my angel book.

"Yes." I'm breathing hard, which makes all my sore places hurt. "You did." I try to control my blushing, but if anything, my face is getting hotter.

"What are you reading?" She flips her finger at my notebook, which I'd slammed down over the angel book. She giggles. "Is it porn?"

I need to take control of this situation. "Yes. I finally cracked Mrs. Wolfe's code and found the porn section in this library."

She picks up my pen and starts playing with it. "What's your e-mail address, Hunter?"

"My what?"

"What's your e-mail? I want to start e-mailing you now that we're . . . friends. Mine is Stardust fourteen at Newmail dot com. What's yours?"

I can't tell her that Stephanie is so cheap she won't let us have a computer. She has a laptop, but we're not allowed to touch it. She says she's protecting us from Internet predators.

I need to think fast here. Stalling, I take out a sheet of paper, careful not to flash my forbidden book. "What's that address again?" While she's repeating and I'm writing, I figure out what I have to do. I know we can get free e-mail accounts from Yahoo here in the media center. The "economically disadvantaged" kids do that. I never bothered to set up an account because I basically had no friends. But now I guess I do.

"I'm Shoehorn six at Yahoo dot com," I say. I'm pretty sure I've picked a handle that nobody would want.

"Shoehorn?" Carolina flips back her curls.

"Uh. It's a private joke. I'd better not explain it to you."

She laughs, touching her perfect tongue to her perfect teeth. "You are so bad, Hunter." Her hand perches on my arm. "I'll see you later, Mr. Shoehorn!"

After I'm done watching her walk away, I see that all the kids in the media center are still staring, obviously wondering how someone like me hooked up with someone like her. *Because I've got friends in high places, chumps!* I reshelve my book and go to Mrs. Wolfe to set up my account.

When I open my locker before fourth period, I see something like confetti. I pick up a few pieces and examine them. It's Drew's entry form in the Kindergarten Queens contest—intercepted, shredded, and delivered. I close the locker door and murmur, "Thank you, Saint Gabriel."

Jessie and I come home to an empty house. I already know that it's the day when Andrea stays late to meet with her geeky service club. There's a note from Stephanie that says she's working late and Drew got picked up at kindergarten by some friend's mom. It's Stephanie's turn to cook but she knows she's going to be exhausted. Will someone order a couple of pizzas?

Stephanie is the only one in our cooking rotation who's allowed to pull that, but I don't care. If she wasn't so lazy, we'd never get anything cool to eat.

Silent from school decompression, Jess and I trudge down the hall to our respective rooms. But then something weird comes over me. I pause at my doorway and ask her, "Do you want to come in and talk?"

She hesitates, like an animal who sees delicious food on the ground but knows there has to be a trap somewhere.

"I need someone to talk to about something." I hear the begging tone in my voice and hate it.

She crosses her arms over her chest. "If it's about you and your skanky girlfriend, I'm not Dear Abby."

Jeez. What will she be like when she's married to some poor slob? "It's not about Carolina, if that's who you were referring to," I say. "It's something else."

She hesitates one more second, but then follows me in. I sit on the bed and she sits on my desk chair. "That is hideous!" She points to my poster of Rolan Thunder.

"No, he's cool!" I tell her. "He's the Bomb from Guam. He's Emotion in Motion. He's the Biggest Deal on the Highlight Reel."

She stares at me like an owl. "Are you sure you belong in Gifted?"

"Let's change the subject. Do you believe in God?"

"Of course I do," she says.

"Like the Official Catholic God?"

"Yes. You know I like to go to Mass whenever I can

drag Stephanie out of bed. Andrea and I both—that's one of the few things we have in common."

"Angels?" I ask. "Do you believe in guardian angels?"

"Sure I do. Where are you going with this?"

I take a deep breath. "I think I'm having a . . . relationship with Saint Gabriel."

The owl-stare narrows to a hawk, then expands again. "That's fine, Hunter. I think that's wonderful. We all need—"

"No, it's more than what you're picturing. I had a Visitation when I was four years old. A real one. I remember it very clearly."

She's still being attentive, but her hands are flexing in a funny way, like she's signaling for help. "I believe you," she says finally. "I've heard stories like that. I think maybe small children receive special grace for that kind of thing."

"Well, now he's trying to come back. The guy at the cemetery, on the motorcycle. That was him."

Her fingers grip the edge of her seat. "Oh, Hunter!"

"Wait. Listen to me. It's the same man. Angel. I recognize him from when I was little. He had that long black hair and . . ."

"Angels do not ride motorcycles."

"How do you know? If they can fly around playing musical instruments, why couldn't they just hop on . . ."

"You're letting your imagination run wild. It's because of Mike's death and how Stephanie is treating you."

"Well, fasten your seat belt. I'm going to tell you some really scary stuff my imagination is doing."

She glances at the door. "Okay."

"I prayed for the ten dollars for Duncan Presser. And it showed up in my locker in this. . . ." I walk to the desk, trying not to notice that she flinches. I take out the envelope and hand it to her.

"You think Saint Gabriel wrote your name on this envelope, put in a ten-dollar bill, snuck into Sawgrass Middle School, and stuck it in your locker?"

Boy, it sounds pretty bad when she tells it. "And then, today, this." I dig in my backpack and take out the contest confetti. "Drew told me she didn't want to be in the contest and I prayed to Saint Gabriel to destroy the entry form and here it is."

"Hunter, you did all this yourself." She looks really scared now.

"Where did I get the ten dollars?"

"I don't know. You tried to get into Stephanie's purse once. Maybe you tried again that same night and pulled it off."

I point to the envelope. "That's not my writing."

She's getting upset, taking short little breaths.

"Maybe you wrote with your left hand. Maybe you're just making all this up to poke fun at me because I'm religious."

"I don't think you're all that religious! I'm showing you a genuine miracle and you're trying to explain it away!"

"Hunter, angels don't work like this! I do believe in angels. I think they can come to your side and comfort you and I think they even rescue people that are lost in the mountains or go to hospitals and miraculously cure people. But I don't think they tear up entry forms and give people money!"

"How do you know?"

"It doesn't sound right!"

We're screaming at each other. I take a deep breath and lower my voice. "What about how my luck has changed lately? What about Carolina Cummings? Can you explain why someone like that would be interested in me?"

She opens her mouth but nothing comes out. She knows this is too much of a miracle to dismiss.

"My luck has totally changed since I started praying. Mrs. Morales is nice to me, you've seen how Duncan leaves me alone on the bus. Now he's picking on Jason Gantner."

"Yeah, but okay, so you started believing in angels

and it gave you confidence and you acted differently. And everyone is reacting to that."

"I think angels are more believable than that kind of touchy-feely psychology crap. If you believe that theory, why don't you walk up to some of the cool kids in your class tomorrow and act like you belong with them and see what happens?"

I had her there. "Hunter, I don't know what to think. I know you've always been a very sensible person. Andrea's the type to go nuts over religion. . . . Hey, how do you know she isn't doing this stuff to you, just to play with your mind?"

That made sense for just a second. "But no, she doesn't know what I'm praying for here in my own room. Unless you've seen her holding a water glass up to the wall."

"No . . . and frankly, I can't imagine her giving you ten dollars either."

We both laugh, but it's the tense kind of laughter you use to pave over something awkward. I'm really sorry I told her.

"I set up an e-mail account today," I say.

You can see the relief flood her face that we've changed the subject. "Yeah?"

"Yeah, my address is Shoehorn six at Yahoo. I thought you might want to know."

"I'm surprised you'd tell me. I thought I was just a pesty little sister to you."

I feel much better now that we're in the awkward place I know. "You're all that and more, Jess. You're my friend. That's why I'm trusting you with this secret. In case I am going off the deep end, you're my witness and you'll know what to tell the guys who come for me with the straitjacket."

She laughs. "You can count on me, Hunter. My . . ." She stops herself and blushes.

"Your what?"

"My address is Hestia thirteen at Yahoo. In case you want to e-mail me."

"I don't know that word."

She looks up all eager and geeky. "Hestia is the Greek goddess of the hearth."

"Oh," I say. "*That* Hestia."

She laughs. "She's my favorite goddess because she's . . . complete within herself. But she's never slipped anything into my locker yet."

Once again, we laugh the ritual laugh.

"Hunter? Do you like Carolina like a girlfriend? You can tell me if it's none of my business."

"It is none of your business, but the answer is, I don't know. I have to get to know her better."

"Do you?" she asks, and then jumps up like the chair burst into flame. "I didn't mean that. Forget I said that."

"Okay. If you'll forget everything I've been saying for the past ten minutes."

"Let's forget I was ever in here at all."

"Deal."

She leaves. Rolan Thunder stares at me from the wall.

The glass in my bedroom window shatters in slow motion, moonlit fragments flying apart like the Big Bang must have looked, and in the center of the explosion is the archangel Gabriel, dressed in black leather, arms spread, his black hair and the fringe on his sleeves fanning out like wings.

I sit up in bed, panting, staring at the intact window. Moonlight glares into my face. I try to tell myself it was just a dream, but I'm awake now. And I hear the roar of the motorcycle outside.

My body jumps out of bed, springs up in one motion, and I run, in my underwear, sprint, tear, fly toward the front door. I have to see. I have to know.

The roar is fainter, getting away. I wrestle with bolts and locks, banging my fingers. I run into the night air, into the moonlight, and see him idling at the corner. The moon edges his black form with silver white, like a mane of electricity. His head is turned toward me. He raises his arm in a wave, or a blessing.

I start running. He turns the corner.

"No!" I scream. "Wait. Please!" My run slows to a defeated jog. The sound of his engine blurs into the traffic and fades completely.

I stand in the street in my neon white underwear. The trees look weird, like they're aware of me, and hostile. I wonder if I'm still dreaming. How can you ever be sure? There's no real test. A dream can simulate anything.

I walk back to my house. My thought is I'll go back to bed and if I see my body lying there, I'll know this is a dream.

I'm cold. The world looks cold in the moonlight. Would a dream-body shiver and feel like it needs to pee?

I open the front door, go in. The VCR is flashing 12:00 like it always does. None of us ever reset the clock after a power failure. I'm careful to relock and rebolt the door because I'm pretty sure I'm not dreaming now. I go to the bathroom and then to my bedroom. No one is in the bed. I lie down. The moonlight seems to burn my face. I fall asleep. In the morning, I have no idea what part of it was real.

Chapter 6

When I get to school the next day, I go straight to the media center to see if Carolina has sent me an e-mail. I'm really surprised to see I have three e-mails waiting for me.

From: stardust14@newmail.com
To: shoehorn6@yahoo.com
Subject: Study date?
Let's get together at your house or my house next week and work on our science project. We can shake things up and see how they settle. Is your house okay? My house is okay but my mom is kind of a pain and if she sees you're a boy she'll get all . . . is your house okay?
Your friend, Carolina
PS: I really like you

I read it over and over, from the explosive word *date* in the subject line to the part about shaking things up, which has to be intentional, to the PS, which in the eighth grade is nothing short of a love poem. I hit reply.

To: stardust14@newmail.com
From: shoehorn6@yahoo.com
Subject: Study date!
I'll bet you anything my foster mom is more of a
pain than your mom, and I have three snoopy
sisters on top of it, but if you can handle all that,
my house is fine. My mom tends to work late on
Mondays, so that might be a good day to shoot for.
YF, Hunter
PS: I really like you too

I delete that PS and try again.

PS: I'm really glad you like me

I delete and try again.

PS: ditto

I delete that PS and leave it off. I hit send. I'm sweating and all the muscles of my back and shoulders are cramped up. This e-mail stuff is intense. I move on to e-mail number two.

From: hestia13@yahoo.com

To: shoehorn6@yahoo.com

Subject: I feel stupid.

I feel stupid sending you an e-mail when we live in the same house, but I thought since we exchanged e-mail addresses, it was rude to not send you one. I'm glad you trusted me with what you told me yesterday. You are the only person in our family that I really respect and I will always feel that way, whatever happens. See you at home. Jessie

I wonder, how many words did she delete before she decided on *respect*? I also wonder what she means by "whatever happens." What's going to happen? I hit reply.

To: hestia13@yahoo.com

From: shoehorn6@yahoo.com

Subject: Yes, but

Will you respect me if the men in the little white coats come for me?

Will you respect me if Stephanie decides she has too many kids and sells me to the gypsies?

Will you respect me if I never, ever get taller than you?

Will you respect me if Carolina becomes my girlfriend?

I hit send fast. I feel feverish from all this. How do people do it every day? I open my third e-mail.

From: guardian2@mindspring.com
To: shoehorn6@yahoo.com
Subject: Hello, Hunter

I hope I'm not frightening you by sending you an e-mail, but I think it's time you heard from me directly. I don't want you to feel you are going crazy or anything like that. I'm real and I'm here and I care about you. I am very sorry for the time I was away from you. I made a promise to you many years ago and I did not keep it. I failed you. But I am here now and all I want to do is make it up to you. Anything in the world you want, Hunter, if it's in my power to do, I will do it for you. I hear your prayers. I will never abandon you again.

Your "guardian angel," Gabriel

PS: Please don't talk about me to other people. They won't understand.

If there's still a media center around me, I'm not aware of it. There's nothing but the screen—white letters on a blue screen, like a starry sky, pulling me in, and beyond that, just a swirl of colors and sounds. I hear a bell ring and wonder if I'm late for class, but I don't really care. All I can do is stare at the screen. Something inside me seems to break loose and I want to cry. He's apologizing to me. An angel is apologizing to me via e-mail and some part of me feels that's absolutely the right thing that should happen. Some weird part of me is sure this all makes perfect sense and that he does owe me something.

"Hunter?" Mrs. Wolfe's voice pulls me back from the edge of something really important I was about to realize.

I panic and hit delete, making Gabriel's message disappear. The moment it's gone, I wonder if it was ever really there. But I couldn't help it, my first impulse was to protect him.

"Yes?" I struggle, in a daze, to focus on Mrs. Wolfe.

"You're late for first period." She points to the clock.

"Yeah." It's like I'm dreaming and I can't wake up.

"I know e-mail is an exciting new toy," she says, "but you have to keep it in its proper place."

I hear the voice of the computer telling me I've got mail. I whirl around and see it's just Jessie, in her reading class, answering me.

"I'll write you a pass," says Mrs. Wolfe. "Go ahead and answer that one and then log off, okay?"

"Okay."

These are Jessie's answers to my four questions. Yes, yes, yes, no.

I sit in the shade of Mrs. Chang's linden tree, eating a bowl of the best fried rice I've ever had. I told her if I had to go home for lunch, I might not be able to get to her lawn this week. Now she's bringing me a refill of my drink: iced ginger tea.

"Here's your money too, Hunter," she says. "I put in something extra because you do such a good job."

"Oh, you didn't need to do that," I say, taking the money out of her hand. "The lunch was great." I hand her back the spoon and bowl, which I have virtually licked clean.

She claps my shoulder with her hand. "Hard to find good boys like you. Want to keep you happy."

I smile up at her, drain my drink, and hand her the glass. "Pretty soon you're going to have to think about getting a new lawn mower. I really can't do my best work with equipment like this."

"New!" Her eyebrows fly up. Here in Leisuretown they hate that word. But then she laughs and shakes her head as she goes into the house. For a good boy like me, she'll consider it.

I yawn, stretch, and check my watch. I start my Saturdays early now—these older people get up before the birds anyway—and that lets me pace myself better through the day.

I still have a few minutes in my self-designated lunch break. I watch a blue jay hopping on the limb above me. He makes a beautiful trilling sound. I didn't know blue jays could make pretty sounds like that. That's what I like about working outdoors. There's a whole different world to see. I take the money Mrs. Chang has given me and put most of it in my pocket for Stephanie but a little bit in my shoe, for me. I know just how much to keep without getting her suspicious. I've decided God helps those who help themselves.

⤙

Carolina shakes the mayonnaise jar and sets it on our laundry-folding table. She spreads her fingers like pink-tipped fans. We watch and wait. Our sedimentary science project is coming along. Most of the substances we tried the first time mixed together too much and didn't stratify. Sand, potting soil, instant coffee, and Jell-O are all worthless. We're now trying fish-tank gravel, kitty litter, beads, tiny ball bearings, and Cheerios.

While we wait for the water to stop swirling, I get to lean in close to Carolina and pretend to watch the jar, but really I look at Carolina's heavy black curls, pulled back today in a ponytail. She's wearing a pink tube top and capris.

"The kitty litter isn't working," she reports. "I guess we don't want to use anything that dissolves. . . ."

I dutifully write that down. "Are you wearing some kind of strawberry perfume?"

"It's lip gloss. Okay, write all this down. The ball bearings dropped immediately, making the first layer. Then the fish-tank gravel. Now the beads and the Cheerios are floating on top of the water, but some of the beads are coming down. So we may get four clean layers. We need to decide on the fifth layer and also figure out what we're learning from this."

I struggle to concentrate. "I feel like we're cheating," I say. "In nature, it's sand and soil and everything that makes the layers."

"Yes, but . . ." She frowns. "I know! It's the time factor! Nature takes thousands of years, maybe millions, to make the stratification and we're doing it in minutes, so we have to compensate by using more obvious things!"

"*Obvious* is the wrong word," I say, scribbling. "But that's the right track. What's the reason we switched to these less-dissolvy things? We knew what to do but why did we do it?" This is the kind of thing Mrs. Morales will love.

"Yeah, this is going to be great when we figure it out." Carolina grabs the edges of her tube top and makes a tugging adjustment. I start wondering what would happen if she hadn't done that and I have trouble focusing on the project again. "Okay, what did we do?

We picked things that didn't dissolve because we don't have the time to let them resettle. . . ."

I've got it. "It's the relative weights of the things!" I write feverishly. "We picked things with very different relative weights, so that they would stratify more quickly and compensate for the time factor!"

"Yes!" Her arms go around me. I wish I could make another discovery right away. "So we can test this theory by adding a fifth element that's either heavier than ball bearings or lighter than Cheerios."

I look at the jar where the Cheerios now slowly absorb water and drift down. "Lighter than Cheerios will be more dramatic. How about feathers? Because they have oil on them and they'll float for a really long time."

"Hunter, you're a genius!" She does it again. I'm lost in a cloud of strawberry fog. My hand touches the silken edge of her ponytail. I decide I need to pull back a little.

"Hunter, we are so going to get an A!" Her face has a beautiful glow.

I feel reckless. "Listen, I've got some money. Let's go to the craft store and get the feathers and then maybe I could take you out for some ice cream or something? Want to?"

"No, I have to get going in a minute. But—we could—I mean, if you're saying you want to go somewhere sometime. . . . I'm not allowed to date, technically, but maybe we could meet at the mall Saturday, by accident. You know?"

No, I don't know anything about this universe, but it sounds wonderful. Then I remember reality. "I have to work all day on Saturday. But Sunday . . ."

"We always visit my grandmother on Sunday."

"Oh." I look at the jar where even the buoyant Cheerios are now stratified.

Then her eyes do something interesting. She sort of tilts her head down and looks up at me through the lashes. "Do you want to kiss me, Hunter?"

If this isn't proof I have a guardian angel, I don't know what is. "Well, sure," I say. "I guess so. I mean, if it's okay with you."

She laughs. "Just do it!"

"Okay." I lean in, she leans in. Strawberry, marshmallow clouds swirl around me . . . and then . . .

"Oh my God!" It's Andrea. Taking in the whole scene with her big, bulging eyes and recording it on her tattletale mental videotape.

"No!" I choke out.

"You filthy little dirtbag!" Andrea says. "Is this what you do when Stephanie works late?"

Carolina acts like she's been in this situation before. Keeping her eyes down, she tugs and smooths herself, slides out of her chair, and scoots past Andrea. Our front door opens and closes.

Meanwhile, I'm still in the strawberry fog and can't think. "Please," I say. "Don't tell Jessie."

"Jessie?" Andrea frowns and I don't know what I meant either. "I'll tell you who I'm going to tell. I'm going to tell Stephanie, so she can whip your ass. That's who I'm going to tell!"

"Listen to me." I can at least think well enough to sit up now. "I've got cash. I'll pay you off. Stephanie doesn't have to know about this. Okay?"

Things aren't bad enough. Now Jessie appears in the doorway. "I just crashed into Carolina! What's going on?"

"He was in here making out with her, the filthy little perv," Andrea says.

Jessie just stares at me, and then she takes off.

"Boy, are you going to get it!" Andrea chuckles.

I get up and run to my room before I give in to the urge to strangle her. I sit on the bed, breathing hard. At first I think I'm going to cry, but instead I feel it go back toward rage. A cold, hard, galvanized rage. I stand up, then I slide to my knees by the side of the bed. I bow my head and pray a simple prayer. "Get her."

Chapter 7

I start the day by answering three e-mails.

To: stardust14@newmail.com
From: shoehorn6@yahoo.com
Subject: Screwed
I'm grounded because of what happened. I'm glad
you're not mad at me—I guess things got out of
hand . . . anyway, I'm glad you're not mad at me.
Your friend, Hunter

To: hestia13@yahoo.com
From: shoehorn6@yahoo.com
Subject: Grow up
Come on, Jess. Cut it out. You're my sister, for God's
sake. Stephanie punished me enough. I don't need you
doing it too. You're my best friend. Please quit acting
like a girl. I can't live in our godforsaken house without
at least one friend. Please. I'm begging. Hunter.

To: guardian2@mindspring.com
From: shoehorn6@yahoo.com
Subject: Prayer

I guess it was wrong to pray for vengeance like that, although if you read Psalms . . . well, I don't need to tell you your business. It's just that, well, you see everything so you must know what happened to me last night. In a family like ours, I think the kids should all stick together, not turn one another in, like Andrea does. I'm not saying I want you to hurt her, but couldn't something happen just to shake her up? So she would think twice about what she does. If it's a sin for me to be asking this of you, let me know. You can never get a straight answer from a priest on stuff like this.

I wait to see if anyone is online and wants to answer. No one does. I put my books in my backpack and hang it off my left shoulder. I'm trying to slip out past Mrs. Wolfe unnoticed, but she has eyes like a hawk.

"Hunter! Why are you holding your arm that way? And what happened to your eye?"

"I was Rollerblading and I fell."

"Oh my goodness. You certainly are accident prone. Didn't something like this happen a couple of weeks ago?"

"Yeah, I tried to jump a fence and hurt my leg."

She's giving me one of those teacher-stares, like she's five seconds from calling Child Protective Services. The funny thing is, though, they never do. "Well, you try to be careful."

"Yes, I will."

About a month after I moved in with Stephanie and Mike, I made a list of one hundred excuses for situations like this. I only used up twelve of them in the first four years. Now that Mike's gone, I'm averaging one a month.

I'm sitting at the kitchen table, trying to get Jessie to talk to me, when Andrea staggers in the front door.

"Oh my God!" Jessie drops her chopping knife and runs to her. "What happened?"

Andrea is a mess. Her hair clip is hanging off one side of her hair, her shirt is twisted sideways, and there's a big hole in her tights that shows a bloody scraped knee.

"A man!" Andrea is clutching her head, holding the door frame with the other hand. "A man tried to . . ."

"Oh my God!" Jessie says.

No, I tell myself. No.

"Sit down," Jessie says. "Hunter, get her a glass of water. Get her a washcloth."

Andrea is trying to gather up her hair, as Jessie pulls

out a chair and forces her down. "Hunter! I said, get her a glass of water!"

I heard her, but I'm having trouble coming out of my daze. I stand up with, like, no idea how to get water. I stare at the sink.

"He was crazy!" Andrea is crying now, holding a fistful of napkins to her face. "He chased me for blocks and blocks. He was riding a motorcycle and he shouted these terrible things at me!"

The glass slips out of my hand and splinters on the floor.

Both girls glare at me. I can see on their faces that they hate me right now, just for being male. Normally, that would make me angry, but at the moment I just feel hugely guilty. I get a broom and dustpan.

"Did you get his license number?"

"He didn't have a license. It was a Honda. He was like a thug, in black leather. Hunter, stop cleaning that up and get me a glass of water!"

"I'll get it." Jessie pushes me away from the sink. "What kinds of things was he shouting? Was it like . . ."

"No." Andrea blows her nose. "It was crazy stuff. Religious things. You know how those fanatics talk. Beware the vengeance of the Lord! A house divided shall not stand! He who troubles his house . . . something about the wind. . . ."

I realize I've cut my hand on the glass. I wait my turn at the sink, dripping.

"How did you get all banged up?" Jessie wets a paper towel and brings it to Andrea, along with her glass of water.

"I fell down. He was chasing me for blocks calling me a Daughter of Babylon and I fell and I thought he was going to . . . do something awful to me, but he just kept circling me on that bike, like a vulture, yelling Bible quotes!"

"We should call the police," Jessie says.

My heart flip-flops. "We better wait and see what Stephanie wants to do," I say. I know Stephanie will quash this. She doesn't want any officers of the court looking at my eye and my arm.

Andrea is sobbing now. "He scared me so bad. He said I'd have to answer at the Throne of God for my hateful ways."

I feel weird. Part of me is really frightened by the fact that I have the power to make something like this happen, but another part of me wants to dance for joy. I don't think it's good to be so confused. A house divided against itself cannot stand.

I feel like I have two choices at this point. A guidance counselor or a priest. I choose a priest, since there's nothing for a guidance counselor to do with a story like mine except have me committed. A priest might too, but at least I think he'll have other options.

Naturally, I don't choose our church. I go to Saint Francis in Margate. I have to cut school, since I'm still grounded. I take two buses to get there, but I know from the newspaper that they serve Mass every day and have two priests, so there's bound to be someone around for me to talk to.

As soon as I see the outside of the church, I think if this angel business eventually turns me into a religious guy, this is the church I'll pick. It has a nice green lawn with a statue of Saint Francis holding his hands out to the birds. There are three statue-birds, cleverly sculpted to look as if they're fluttering around him, and then two real birds, a dove and some kind of blackbird, sitting on his head. I like a saint who's the outdoor type, like me.

I push open the doors and go past the foyer with a tableful of fund-raising literature and pass into the dark, magical part of the church, where the candles are flickering away and old ladies are going through their paces—

stand, sit, kneel, mutter, cross, exit. People should be nicer to old ladies. They're the only ones who bother to come out and pray for people. Mowing all these lawns has made me think how nice it would be to have grandparents. The kids at school make fun of their grandparents because they can take them for granted, but I'd love to adopt one of these little praying ladies and take her out for ice cream.

When I see the altar, I know I've picked, or been guided to, the right place. There's a flying Jesus behind the altar and all around him are angels. On his right is clearly Michael, because he has a sword and a mean look on his face. On his left is my man, Gabriel, holding a flower. Once again, they've made the mistake of portraying him blond. Up above Jesus' head is a third angel in flight, looking down on the church with a sweet expression. He's got something that looks like a fishing pole in his hand. I figure he must be Raphael. I stand there awhile, sort of soaking the angels in, and then I look for some kind of side exit. I have to explore a couple of different hallways because this is a big church, but finally I hit pay dirt—a library full of books and a young priest sitting on a window ledge, reading. I'm really happy I caught him this way and not in his office.

"Father?"

He looks up and then looks nervous. Probably he figures I'm a parishioner he's supposed to recognize.

I keep walking toward him, like I have confidence in myself. "My name is Hunter LaSalle. I don't go to your church but I was hoping you could talk to me. I mean, I probably should have called first or come to confession but I really want to just talk. You know?"

He kind of smiles and puts his book down. He holds out his hand. "I'm Father Ruiz. Would you like to see if Father McClure is free to talk to you? He's senior here. I'm just a rookie."

"No—I'd really rather it was someone . . . your age."

He laughs and then frowns again. He probably thinks this will be about sex. "Let's go to my office, Hunter."

His office is so small he can hardly crowd himself behind the desk, which is a mess. On the wall behind him is a gigantic oil painting of the Madonna. She and her baby glare at me.

"So." Father Ruiz folds his hands on the desk. "What brings you here today, Hunter?"

I realize there's no gentle way to ease into this. "What do you think about angels, Father?"

"Angels?" I'm used to this counselor's trick. They stall to get you to say more. I stay silent.

"Are you a Catholic, Hunter?"

I guess he has to be careful what he says so he won't violate my civil rights. "I don't go to Mass, but I'm Catholic."

"You were raised in a Catholic home?"

Here we go. I always hate telling my sad story. "I wasn't really raised at all. I've lived in four foster homes and an orphanage. Two of the homes were Catholic, including the one I'm in now. I can't tell you about my birth family."

"I'm sorry. I'm just trying to understand the situation, Hunter. If you have a theology question, why aren't you asking your parish priest?"

Baby Jesus looks at me, like, *Yeah, what's wrong with you?* I avoid his gaze.

"I don't want my family to know. . . . Can I just tell you what's happening to me?"

He sits back. "Sure."

"I think I'm being contacted by an angel."

His dark eyes remain steady and calm, but one of his hands clenches up a little. "Contacted? You mean like a Visitation?"

"Yes. Do you think that's possible?"

"I . . . believe it's possible as an article of faith, but I don't think it happens a lot. Tell me about your Visitation."

"It's more than one. He's sort of . . . harassing me, like he's trying to strike up a relationship. I have a real fuzzy memory of when I was really little—right before my birth mother gave me up—that was the first time I saw him. He came into my room and talked to me."

Father Ruiz is breaking training now, leaning forward, getting interested. "What did he look like?"

"Long black hair . . ."

"Male? Or without gender?"

"He seemed like a male. He had a male voice. And black wings."

"Black wings?"

"I think so. Like, black feathery wings. When I first saw him they were spread out, but I think he folded them up later. . . . I'm not positive about this stuff. I was, like, four."

"Are you positive it wasn't a dream?"

"No, I know I was awake."

"Four-year-olds don't always know the difference between fantasy and reality."

I sit back. "But now I'm thirteen. And he's back."

"He's back?"

"He's back. My foster father died and this guy—this angel—came to the cemetery on a motorcycle. . . ."

"Whoa, whoa, whoa. On a motorcycle?"

"Yes, Father. He stopped a couple of yards from the funeral and he stared at me and I recognized him. And now, when I pray for things to happen, they happen. I think he's protecting me and I want to know—do you think this is possible? Do you think an angel could work this way?"

He hesitates a long time. "Two things," he says finally. "**First,** you have to understand where I'm coming from. I'm a priest. It's my duty to defend—to uphold the mysteries of the world. We live in a time, Hunter, when people don't believe in anything they can't buy or sell. I became a priest because I don't agree with that. I believe—I feel—that there are angels and saints and a Heaven. You came to me for a reason. So you already know I'm going to say, Yes, Hunter, I think something like this is possible."

He said *two* things so I wait.

"But . . . even though I'm a priest, I'm just a human being, like you, Hunter. There are many, many stories like yours of Visitations and even help and rescue from angels. I believe at least some of them are true. Nothing like that has ever happened to me, and I wasn't there when it happened to you. So I have to tell you in all humility . . . I don't know what to think. I don't know if you are wishing this into being or if an angel has singled you out for a special blessing. You'll have to pray about it and decide for yourself."

I'm disappointed, but I have to like his honesty. "Isn't there some kind of test you guys can do, to investigate?"

He makes a face. "Well, kind of, but if we go down that road, Hunter, you're going to have a whole crowd of people in your front yard wanting to be healed and helped by the 'angel boy.' You'll be on the news. People will try to exploit you. I'm not speaking for the Church now, I'm just telling you man-to-man. If this is a genuine experience, it should be a private matter between you and God. You seem like a pretty smart kid. You can figure this out."

"My whole life has changed since it happened. I used to be the biggest loser in the world and now I get everything I want."

"Let me ask you another question, Hunter. Are you in a position to do good?"

"Sir?"

"I'm trying to make an explanation for myself of why this would happen. Maybe this angel is beckoning to you because you're in a position to do some kind of good. Right some wrong, perhaps, or help someone less fortunate than yourself. If this were my situation, I'd be asking, Why is this happening to me?"

Almost as if guided, my mind goes to Stephanie. "If I know of someone—and I think they're—well—evil? Could it be that? Could it be that my angel wants me to fight the evil?"

He frowns again. "You have to be very careful with this, Hunter. You have to pray very hard for guidance and you have to know the difference between your will and God's will. If you have a power, or a gift of some kind, a lot of responsibility goes with it."

"Yes, sir."

"Let's pray together now."

I lower my eyes because I'm embarrassed.

"Father, guide Hunter here to know your will and to clearly understand you. Protect him from false ideas and thoughts, and if you have chosen him for a special blessing, help him to understand what it is. If he needs your protection, please grant it to him in the name of the Father, the Son, and the Holy Spirit. Amen."

I look up at him. "Come back and talk anytime you want to, Hunter. I think you should have someone to talk about this to. And also . . ." He actually blushes.

"What?"

"I want to know the outcome of this for myself. Okay?"

I smile at him. "Okay."

I practically bump into walls on my way out of the

church. I feel so weird. I really, really liked him and thought he handled my questions just right, but when he was praying, it was as if my whole mind went into white noise. I'm still in a daze as I walk into the street. My brain feels like a computer that got knocked off-line by a power surge.

Chapter 8

When I get home, Stephanie is pitching a fit. Happily, she isn't pitching it at me.

"Yes! You can go look it up right now and I'll hold!" She paces up and down the room, her red nails clawed around the portable phone.

I see that all three of my sisters have gathered just outside her pacing range and are staring at her anxiously, which makes me realize it isn't some co-worker or client she's mad at—it's something to do with us.

She lectures us while she's on hold. "This is the way the world works, guys. If you take things lying down, people will screw you for all you're worth. You have to speak up, ask questions, get in somebody's face, and make damn sure— What?" she says to the receiver. "Never received it? That's not possible. That's just not possible."

Drew looks like she's either going to cry or pee. Jessie

is staring straight at me, her eyes like blue torches. Then I get it. Stephanie is talking to the magazine that sponsored the Kindergarten Queens contest. I sweep the room for more info and see the current issue of the magazine splayed in the corner of the room, where Steph must have hurled it when she saw Drew didn't win. I wonder if I can sneak past everyone and get to my room.

"You check again! Don't check your computer! You go through all the entry forms by hand and you call me back! I'll go to the papers and tell them you rigged the goddamn thing! You probably threw away all the entries from the white kids to make sure a minority kid would win. I know how you people operate."

I'm getting a headache. Stephanie is listening now. She gets a pen. "Okay, I want that person's name and your name and your supervisor's name. The publisher's name I'll get from your masthead. And if I don't hear from you, don't worry, you will definitely hear from me!" She punches the disconnect and stops pacing so fast her hair whirls into her face. She looks at us, trying to figure out how to work off the rest of her rage. Drew starts to cry quietly.

"Stephanie," says Jessie. "There's something I think you should know."

Even then, I don't get it. I just look at her, wondering why she would want to draw fire.

Stephanie's mad at her hair now, raking it out of her face with both hands. "What?!"

"That contest never did get the entry form. Hunter took it out of the mailbox and tore it up."

"Yay, Hunter!" Drew jumps up and down and claps.

Stephanie, like me, is paralyzed at this unexpected turn of events. "Hunter? Jessie, what are you talking about?"

I can hardly hear them over the din of my mind screaming, *Why, Jessie, why?* Would she really sell me out because she's jealous of some girl? Deliberately betray me like this? Break four years of trust between us and hand me over to this madwoman?

"I'm worried about him," Jessie rushes on. "He wasn't in school today. I think that he's losing his sense of . . ."

"Did you cut school?" Stephanie asks me. I guess the other crime is too overwhelming for her to process.

I notice how Andrea is smiling. This is front row seats at the Garden for her. She gets to see me killed and her hands aren't even dirty.

"I went and talked to a priest," I say. "I'm having trouble handling Mike's death." I look at Jessie. *There, you bitch! Game, set, and match.*

"He showed me the pieces of the entry form. They're in an envelope in his room!"

"It's my fault!" Drew jumps in. "I told him to do it! I don't want to be a queen, Mommy. I don't want to!"

Stephanie is moving toward me slowly now, a predator.

"I didn't!" I hold up both hands. "I swear to you, Stephanie. I did not tear up that form."

"Look in his room!" Jessie's face is pinched with hatred. She looks like a rodent. "Look in his desk!"

The rest of the scene isn't very pretty.

I remember when I first came to Mike and Stephanie's house, four years ago. I was nine and this was the fourth home they were trying me in. In my first placement, which I hardly remember, the woman left after about a week of taking care of me and the caseworker didn't like that I was sleeping in the same bed as the man. I was only four and my memories are foggy, but I'm pretty sure there was nothing wrong with the poor guy. He was drinking a little, but I think he just missed his wife and wanted somebody there in the room with him, like a dog or something. Maybe I'm blocking out a terrible memory, like about a hundred counselors have tried to tell me, but I really don't think so. I always look back and think how that lonely guy and I might have made it work.

Then I went to the House from Hell. Their name was Fairbanks or Fairfax. They had this older kid, Toby.

He was probably ten, but to me he looked like a twenty-year-old longshoreman. Toby's first words to me were, "This is MY yard!" And it was. Toby was one of those cute kids who torture neighborhood dogs and cats, and I was just another small mammal to him. He tied me up with ropes in the garage, tried to bury me alive in the backyard, and gave me a seven-stitch cut in the back of my head while we were playing pro-wrestlers and he'd found a folding chair in the hall closet. His parents never did anything to him because he was their real kid and I was just an experiment that could be canceled. I pleaded with the caseworkers to get me out of there and after enough trips to the hospital, they agreed with me. They wrote in my file that I wasn't integrating with the family, as if *I'd* done something wrong. The caseworker warned me that if I got too many placements, nobody would ever want me because I'd look like a problem child.

By that time I was seven and I didn't get my hopes up anymore. I spent the next two years with Lily Stevens. I know her first name because she wanted me to call her Lily. Lily was a good person, but she was completely crazy. There were about a hundred things you had to remember to keep up with her craziness, but the main thing was not to generate garbage. The planet was in danger if we put out more than one little sack of trash per week. Aluminum foil had to be washed and reused. Same for plastic bags. She thought I was separating plies in the toilet paper to make it last, but since she didn't follow me into the bathroom, I drew the line there. She was very cheap and everything she had was from yard sales and didn't work right. None of the clocks kept time. I wore weird clothes to school and got beat up regularly—no big deal for me at that point. The worst thing she did was serve food she knew was spoiled. Ever see a rubber carrot that you can wobble back and forth? Ever try to choke down an overripe banana? Occasionally, she'd miscalculate and I'd throw up, but again, this was all stuff I was willing to work with. But one day when a caseworker was visiting, Lily just started crying. Started crying and couldn't stop. Started talking about all the assassinations that happened when she was a kid, Kennedy and King and Kennedy and how her mother never let her wear stockings, only tights, and pretty soon, the caseworker pulled the plug and made a phone call.

So I ended up here. This family was like the Brady Bunch after what I'd been through. Mike was the most reasonable, decent guy you could find, and when Stephanie flew off the handle, he would jump in to protect me, at least, most of the time. I got the feeling after a while that he was the one who had wanted me. They already had the girls, including Drew, who was just a baby then. At first, Andrea and Jess were a solid wall of opposition to me, making dumb-boy jokes, and I knew Stephanie felt the same, that male children contained evil chemicals that would destroy the civilized world of girls.

Still, life was okay here until Mike died. Jessie defected from Andrea and became my ally, or so I thought. Drew, when she's not obnoxious, is a pretty sweet kid. Andrea, I could always handle.

But today, as I lie on my bed with a set of new bruises on top of last week's bruises, calculating how many days I'll have to stay out of school until I look all right and trying not to play the memory tape of how it looks and feels to have a woman beating you down when you're supposed to be turning into a man—I think to myself, if I call CPS right now and show them my arms and my jaw and my back, I'm out of here. They don't visit anymore because our situation has been "stable" for so many years. Those caseworkers are overloaded and any kid they can let slide, they let slide. But if I called them—or the cops, for that matter—I could get my revenge on Stephanie right now.

I pray about this to Saint Gabriel as I lie on my back, holding a package of frozen peas against my jaw. I pray to him and tell him he needs to help me figure this thing out. I don't want to be Stephanie's punching bag anymore, and I sure don't want to explode someday and start giving it back to her. But do I want to get thrown back into the foster-care pool again? I'm a thirteen-year-old boy, the most unwanted commodity in the child market.

"You're an angel, you figure it out," I say, and close my eyes, hoping the pain will let me sleep.

When I get back to school, at the end of the following week, I find there are no e-mails for me, either from Heaven or Earth. I send one to Saint Gabriel that bounces back in five seconds from the Mailer Daemon (note irony) saying there is no one at that address. My guardian angel has moved, left no forwarding address. I feel like I'm going to cry, right there in the media center, and then this really weird, spooky thought occurs to me. What if I imagined everything? That's what Jessie thinks. What if I'm really cracking up? I don't have any real evidence there was ever an angel in my life. Maybe I'm like one of those people on truTV who goes into a trance and does stuff and forgets about it, like the guy I just saw who claimed he murdered his wife while he was sleepwalking. Maybe I took the ten dollars out of Stephanie's purse and put it in my own locker. Maybe I did tear up the entry form. Maybe I'm like that guy in *A Beautiful Mind* who can't tell what's really happening and what's in his head. Except for the guy at the cemetery, whom everybody saw, and The Motorcycle Man, who chased after Andrea, I've got no evidence at all. Maybe Jessie is really the best friend I've got, trying to help me because she sees the road I'm going down. My whole body is sort of trembling, like puppies do. If you're that crazy, they do serious stuff to you. Maybe I should tell all this to a counselor, but what if they lock me up this very day in some hospital and never let me out? Maybe I could talk to Father Ruiz again. I hope I haven't imagined *him*.

I feel a sharp pain in my sore arm. I look up and see the jungle of Carolina's curls as she sits down next to me. She's managed to punch me right on a bruise, but when I see her, I forgive her. Her eyes are like blue sparklers and she smells like Coca-Cola today—those flavored lip glosses will kill you.

"Hi, Hunter," she says in this weird girly voice she never used before.

I rub my arm. "Hi."

"When can we get together and work on science again?" Her face even looks different. It's that morphing-into-a-woman thing again. So scary. She leans in a little closer. The smell of cola is kind of overpowering.

"I'm . . . uh . . . grounded right now. Because of what happened. My sisters ratted me out to my foster mother."

"Oh." She tosses curls over her shoulder. "You *were* a very bad boy!"

Huh? We barely even kissed and it was definitely mutual. Okay, I know this is some kind of flirting behavior. I know I'm supposed to want to be a bad boy, but it's not working for me at the moment. I'm tired and sore and if it weren't for Carolina, Jesse probably wouldn't have ratted me out. "One of us should write up our notes on the experiment," I say. "You have a laptop at home, right?"

She's mad. Her eyes shift somehow. You'd think living with three girls and a psychotic woman would make me able to understand the species. But I don't. "I'm not doing your work for you, if that's what you think!" she says. "And there's another thing I think you should know. Steve Richie has been looking at me. I think he likes me. So I don't think you want to be grounded for too long."

Now I'm mad. I'm really mad at Jessie and Stephanie and my unreliable angel, but Carolina is the one in front of me. "It's not my *choice* to be grounded," I say. "And if you like Steve Richie better than me, go for it! Tell him I wish him luck!"

Okay, that was a little angrier than I wanted. She stands up. "I'm getting myself a new lab partner too. Your experiment is lame!"

"I thought it was our experiment!" I say. "But I guess I was wrong."

A few heads are turning in our direction. She picks up her books. "I'm just glad I found out what you're really like!" she says. "I thought you were nice!" Somehow in whirling to leave she manages to catch my sore arm one more time with her notebook. I think girls have some kind of radar for finding wounds.

I can't win even with the angels on my side.

The bus lets us off. The Skylark Pest Control van is still across the street. One of those houses must have a big problem. As usual, Jessie marches into the house silently, ahead of me. As usual, Andrea isn't there. What do they do to you in high school that you never get home on time? I consider telling Jessie I broke up with Carolina, but I don't really want to give her the satisfaction. I check the refrigerator door to make sure it's not my night to cook and spread my homework on the kitchen table. I'm just starting to concentrate when I hear the car. Over the engine and through a solid door, I hear Drew, her voice rising and falling like a British ambulance. Knowing Drew, this could be anything from a major injury to some kid taking her favorite crayon. I open the back door to see if I can help and Drew hurls herself against my legs. "Stop her, Hunter! Don't let her give me to a man! She wants to give me to a man!"

I look to Stephanie, who is wearily dragging her blazer and laptop from the back seat. I know this can't be right. If anything, Stephanie would *sell* Drew to a man.

"Look how she runs to you!" Stephanie's eyes stab me as she walks past. "You've completely undermined my authority around here."

I don't rise to the bait. I'm still healing. "What's going on?" I try to pry Drew off my legs.

"I'll explain it to you." Steph is still shedding baggage. "Drew, go to your room, now!"

"Nooooo! Hunter, stop her! I don't want to go to that man!"

Stephanie grabs Drew's arm and wrenches her off me so hard I almost fall. "He is not your father!" she shrieks. "But I AM YOUR MOTHER!" She punctuates this last sentence with four loud smacks on Drew's butt. She's never hit Drew or any of the girls before.

Drew's hands fly to her backside and a sort of delayed-reaction howl comes out of her mouth.

"You go to your room now or I'll really fix you!" Stephanie fakes a move toward Drew, who runs away, still holding herself. Her door slams like a gunshot. I'm amazed all this racket hasn't brought Jessie out of her room, but I guess she's sulking too loud to hear anything.

"What are you staring at?" Stephanie asks me, even though I'm not. "Don't you think she needs some discipline? She's completely spoiled, thanks to you."

I get a spooky feeling she's talking to Mike, not me. I'm not the only crazy one in the house, after all.

"What's she so upset about?"

Stephanie sits down heavily at the kitchen table. "I'm still determined that she have a modeling career, despite your sabotage. Some little girls would be thrilled. . . ."

"But what set her off today?"

She rummages in her purse and shows me a classified she's torn out of the paper.

MODEL SEARCH—LOOKING FOR ADORABLE GRLS, 5–14. PHOTO LAYOUTS, PORTFOLIO QUALITY. HAVE CONTACTS IN NY AND HLLYWD. HUGE $$$$ IF THE RIGHT LOOK. LIVING DOLLS STUDIO 954-555-6636.

While I struggle to choke down a gasp of horror, Stephanie is still talking. "I called the number and the man said a girl Drew's age could make a lot of money if she had the right pictures. She spends a whole day in the studio with him, and then we only buy the prints we like."

"And the Internet buys the prints you don't know

about! Stephanie, are you crazy? Do you really not know it's not safe to give a little five-year-old as pretty as Drew to some strange guy to take pictures of her? Are you allowed to be there?"

"No, but he explained that stage mothers—and I guess that's what I am now—can upset the kids and mess up the shots. It just figures with your little adolescent boy mind you'd assume it was something dirty. Are you looking at things like that on the Internet?"

My whole body is sweating. "Stephanie, this is important. You have to understand. This is a bad man. He wants to take bad pictures of Drew and sell them to other bad men. This kind of story is on the news all the time. You must have heard of things like this."

"What I've heard is that you can't break into modeling unless you have good head shots and I can't take competitive pictures of Drew here at home. If this man was doing something illegal, he wouldn't advertise in the paper."

"Did you see all the escort service ads? Did you see all the massage parlor ads?"

"You filthy . . . how do you know about things like that? What's wrong with you?"

I look into her eyes and try to understand. Is she so wrapped up in her dream of Drew the baby-supermodel that she won't look at the truth? Or does she know perfectly well what this is and she just doesn't care because she thinks there's money in it?

"Stephanie, please. Don't do this. Drew doesn't want to and it's dangerous. You can't leave her alone with a person like this. He might hurt her. She's just a little girl. You have to protect . . ." Suddenly out of nowhere I break down and cry. Why isn't there anyone to protect us? We're children. We have no power. If Stephanie really wants to do this, there's nothing I can do to stop her. I put my head on my arms.

"Hunter," she says almost kindly. "You're tired. You're not thinking clearly. Don't you think the police would arrest him if he were doing something wrong? Do you think I'd put my little girl in jeopardy?"

I don't even pick up my head or stop crying. "I wish Mike was here!" I wail.

When I finally look up, she's gone.

Chapter 9

I come home Saturday afternoon tired, sweaty, rich, and happy, because Saturday has turned into my favorite day of the week. On Saturday, I get to live in another world from the twin horror shows that are my family and school. I'm outside all day. I'm earning money and feeling good about myself. I've started saving up from the money I skim and don't give to Stephanie. With today's take, I'll have over a hundred dollars. I don't know what I'm saving for. Maybe I'm dreaming of running away.

The Skylark Pest Control van is parked on our street again. Boy, there must really be some kind of gigantic infestation going on, but you expect things like that in south Florida. I'm glad Stephanie is such a stickler for cleanliness. I haven't seen anything weird around our house, except the human inhabitants.

The sun is just setting as I fit my key in the lock, and

I feel myself breathing deeply and just enjoying life. I want to hesitate here forever on the threshold, but hunger makes me go inside.

The first thing I notice is that the house is too quiet. Also, no lights are on. Usually, the minute the sun gets low in the sky, Stephanie shuts the drapes and turns the lamps on. She can't stand the time when the light is fading. And the house *feels* wrong. I stand perfectly still, almost afraid to move, like a deer stepping from a clearing and sniffing for predators.

I hear a funny little sound coming from the kitchen. A soft clinking rattle that comes every few seconds, but not at regular intervals you can count off. I just keep listening, trying to identify as the sun gets lower and the western windows pour this deep orange light across me.

Rattle-clink. Rattle-clink. Drinking. Someone is drinking back in the kitchen. Stephanie is drinking and there is no sign of my sisters.

My arms and legs turn to ice. I've watched a lot of truTV over the years. Stephanie is capable of anything. My mind goes to teen horror flicks and I picture a different sister in every room, lying in pools of blood, Stephanie waiting for me to come home for the coup de grâce. Still, I'm paralyzed, not knowing what to do. Should I run to the neighbors for help? What if this is all my imagination and nothing is wrong? What if it's not? I reach behind me for the doorknob.

"Hunter? Come here. I've got something you'll want to see."

Her voice sounds perfectly reasonable. Yeah, just like Jack Nicholson in *The Shining*. What's she got to show me? An ax from the garage?

I hear footsteps coming and my legs prickle. My knees get weak and I go down like a lame horse. Ruby red light bathes me from all directions.

She stands, a black silhouette in the brightness. "What's wrong with you? Are you all right? Did you get too much sun?"

She sounds like a mother. Like a concerned mother. I look up, trying to find her face. She puts some things she's holding down on the floor and comes to me. "Hunter, answer me. Are you sick?"

Yes, yes, I'm mentally ill. I'm seeing angels and murderers everywhere. Help me. "I just felt faint for a second. That's all." I struggle to stand. "Where is everybody?"

She gives a little laugh. "As if you didn't know." She goes and turns on a lamp. I see that what she's set on the floor is a sheaf of papers, the long court kind, and a cocktail. She has raccoon eyes from crying. I creep to the couch, holding the edges of it. "What happened? Where are the girls?"

Her laugh is almost a cough. "They left with the social worker who's coming back tonight to talk to you. You won, Hunter. It took you four years to destroy my family, but now you've done it." She goes and retrieves her drink and the papers. She keeps the drink, gives the papers to me. I'm very familiar with these kinds of documents. Scanning them quickly, I see that a social worker was tipped off and came out to investigate our home and decided to take the girls on the spot. I play in my mind the familiar scene of how you get loaded into a strange car and taken off to who knows where for your next adventure. It's terrifying. I think of Drew and want to cry.

Stephanie sits on the couch facing me. She didn't close the drapes and the windows turn into mirrors, reflecting both of us from several directions.

"What are the charges or grounds or whatever?" I ask.

"What you told them. That I was physically abusive and sexually exploitive. Sweet little Jessie started pounding the nails in the minute the caseworker got here, telling her about the photographer I wanted to send Drew to, making me sound like some kind of goddamn child pornographer when all I wanted was for Drew to have a modeling career! Andrea kept her mouth shut, God bless her, but Jessie said I was physically abusive and they found this tiny little bruise on Drew's butt from that tap I gave her the other day and that was enough to bury me. Of course, if you'd been here it would have been even worse, since no one understands how hard it is to control a boy your age without a father around, but hey, no one is interested in my side of the story. That was obvious from the start. The fact that I've taken care of all you ungrateful little demons all these years—that was worth nothing. Anyway, someone's coming at seven and then you get to leave the wicked witch's castle too."

I can't believe it. I can't believe my sisters are gone. This is the longest I've been in any home, and even though Stephanie *is* the wicked witch, where will I go now? I'll probably never see my sisters again. I could end up anywhere, or worse, stuck in some group-home limbo until I turn eighteen. My eyes fill up and tears spill out.

"Save it!" she hisses, taking a big gulp. "This is what you wanted, isn't it? When you called CPS? How did you do it? From a pay phone? Did you disguise your voice?" She looks at her glass and frowns, gets up and staggers to the kitchen. I listen to her making her next drink. I wonder how many she had before I got home. I wonder who called CPS. Maybe Jessie. Then I sort of shiver and wonder if it was me. Maybe I'm really in bad shape and I'm doing all these things and blaming it on some guardian angel in my mind. It's so creepy. I try to force myself to remember if I went inside any of the houses today. If I asked to use the phone.

"How do you know Jessie didn't do it?" I call out.

"The caseworker kept asking me if I had a boyfriend. So I know they got an anonymous tip from a man. Can you believe it? I told her I'm a widow and she's got a lot of nerve asking me if I've got a boyfriend. Then she wants to know how recently Mike died because obviously they want to make a case that I'm a grieving psychopath!"

That would be a good case to make, I think.

"They all look alike, don't they?" she calls over the rattle of ice cubes. "Those drab little social workers. You've probably seen more of them than I have. Can't they dress properly? I mean, it's not a question of money. You can put together a decent outfit at Target if you want to. I used to do it, back when. They don't have to wear those ratty cardigan sweaters. They could get a nice cotton jacket, even a polyester one. Anything but those droopy sweaters. I swear, I'm watching her fill out her ten million papers and that droopy, disgusting sweater kept sliding off her shoulder until I wanted to KILL her!"

I look at the clock. Fifteen minutes to seven. It won't be hard to get me out of here, what with Stephanie's drinking herself into a stupor and the bruises I can show.

I wonder if Stephanie would freak if I just slid down to my room and threw a couple of things into a duffel. When they go back for your things, they always miss something important.

"Everything was so perfect before we got you," she continues. She's not really talking to me anymore. "We had the perfect family. Andrea and Jessie were so sweet in those days. I used to dress them up in these little Ralph Lauren dresses and take them to church. We could afford things like that back then. Then we adopted the baby and I was so happy. Drew was so beautiful. I almost felt like she was really mine." I hear glass shatter in the kitchen. Stephanie explodes into curses.

I decide to wait for the social worker from the locked safety of my room. I stand up.

"Where do you think you're going?" She's practically on top of me. "I'm talking to you! I want to tell you how that bastard Mike ruined my life just because he wanted a boy!"

I knew it. I always knew it. Mike wanted me and she didn't. I really want to get to my room. It's five to seven, but social workers tend to run late.

"Why don't you lie down?" I ask, putting a few steps between us. "You've had a really tough . . ."

She lunges, her claws digging into my collar. I try to break loose by running, but that just pulls me off my feet and swings me to the floor. She gets on me like a school-yard bully, knees pressing into my chest, screaming in my face. "From day ONE you were trouble!" The heel of her hand slams the side of my head. I see pretty fire-works.

The hell with this. She's not my mom anymore. She's just some nut I've had enough of. I grab her hair and pull hard, yanking her off balance. She slides to the side and I scramble up and run, but she chases me into the hallway and kicks me, I think. Something sharp hits me in the kidney and I double over. "I knew you were a bad kid!" she screams, punching me all over. "Those other homes threw you out. I told Mike you would ruin everything. You . . ." It deteriorates into nothing but swearing and random explosions of pain. I can't find a way to get free.

Then we're on the floor again. I realize as her hands go for my throat that she thinks she has nothing to lose and just a couple of minutes to get her revenge on the kid who ruined her life. I thrash like a panicky fish on a hook, break her hold on my neck, and scream, "Saint Gabriel! Help me! Help me!"

The front door crashes open.

Chapter 10

Haloed by lamplight. I see the gigantic man, black wings swirling as he rushes toward us. No, it isn't wings. It's the leather fringe on his jacket. His long blue black hair, his face. His eyes. This is the man I saw at the cemetery, the man who came to me when I was four. He's real. He's *real*.

He wrenches Stephanie off me and throws her like a sack of laundry. Her body hits a wall and slides down. "Hunter, are you okay?" he asks me.

I'm incapable of speech. I'm sure I'm not hallucinating, but how do I know? Maybe she choked me into another episode. But no, he's real. I don't know what he is, but he's real and he knows me and he's here to rescue me. I make a croaking sound.

Meanwhile Stephanie has staggered up and throws herself on his back like a cougar. He lurches around and they go down together. I can't move and I don't know what I'd do if I could.

Stephanie is screaming at him and trying to use her claws on his face, but he's very big and strong and he gets her down and sort of straddles her. I feel sick. "Don't fight him!" I call out in my croaky voice. "He's too strong!"

He has her by the throat now and is sort of shaking her and saying, "Stop it, stop it."

Then everything comes to a stop. Stephanie comes to a stop. I turn my head and throw up on the rug. The house is very quiet. He lets go of her neck and stands up. "Hunter," he says. "I didn't have any choice."

"Who are you?" I say. "What are you?"

"We have to get out of here now," he says, looking around. "Your social worker will be here any second. Come on."

I'm just barely able to sit up. My whole body is shaking. Different voices are shouting in my head, telling me different things to do. Go with him. Don't go with him. "You . . ."

"Come on, we don't have time." He picks me up, fireman style, and we're out in the twilight, him racing with me, me bouncing on his shoulder. I hear his panting breath, smell his fear. He's human. He's human and I don't know who he is or what he wants.

"Help!" I scream to the whole neighborhood. "Help me!"

"Oh, God, no, Hunter, don't!" He's running to the van, Skylark Pest Control, and he slides the side panel open and throws me in. I collide with his motorcycle and what looks like a lot of sound equipment. The word *surveillance* surfaces in my mind. This man has been stalking me. I drag myself to the panel door, but the engine has already started and we scream off into the night.

⌐⌐

The song plays over and over, a woman's voice like an angel, but the song is oppressive, a slow, trudging melody with a horrible edge of fear in it. A language I don't know. He plays it 24–7, here in his hovel, where I'm now a prisoner, locked in a bathroom so small I can barely stretch my legs out. It's like a song you'd play in a movie if some guy was walking the last mile to the electric chair. And that's how I feel. Doomed.

The bathtub has rust stains and drips continuously. There are several cracked floor tiles. The medicine cabinet is low on hygienic products, high on prescription meds. I wonder where I am, what time it is, whether the social worker ever came and if she did, did she find Stephanie's body? Maybe they'll assume I snapped and killed her. That would be great, because then the police would be trying to find me.

The music cycles again, like Chinese water torture. I want to bang my head on the floor, knock myself out to make it stop.

The lock springs on the door and I jump up as he comes in. He has a bowl of some kind of muck with a spoon stuck in it. I guess he doesn't plan to murder me if he's feeding me. But that still leaves a whole range of other horrible things he might want.

"Tell me who you are and what you've been doing to me with all this angel stuff," I say.

"I will, I promise," he says. His eyes are very kind, but I keep the image of him choking Stephanie fresh in my mind. "Are you hungry, Hunter?"

I sit down on the only available furniture. I feel suddenly very weak. "How do you know my name?"

"I've always known your name. I've known you all your life."

"Don't give me any of that angel shit, mister, because I'm not a genius about religion, but angels don't stalk people and kill their parents. I'm almost positive."

"I had to do certain things. . . ."

"Tell me how you did it. Was my room bugged?"

"Yes. I needed to know what was going on in that house."

I remember the day I thought Andrea had disturbed things in my room. Shortly after that my guardian angel started knowing what I was praying for. "Where was the bug?"

"Behind that picture of the wrestler."

Rolan Thunder. I felt like he'd been trying to tell me something. "And you parked that van on my street and listened."

"Yes."

"And you were"—I almost choke with anger—"answering my prayers, putting stuff in my locker at school, following me everywhere . . . e-mailing me."

"I decided to cut that short. I wasn't sure if you could trace me that way. Hunter, you have to understand why—"

"No! I don't. You've kidnapped me. You've been taking advantage of me ever since my father died and you showed up at his funeral."

"He wasn't your father." He offers me the bowl. "Why don't you try some of this?"

The door is open. I wonder if I just surprise him and run for it, how far could I get? No. Better wait for a really good opportunity. He can't guard me forever.

"I did everything to protect you, don't you see? I didn't like what those people were doing to you."

"But you made me think I was going crazy. Pretending to be my guardian angel—"

"But I am, Hunter. In a way I am." He can see I'm

not going to accept the muck, which appears to be canned beef stew. He sets it on the floor, and, immediately, a big fluffy cat pushes her way in and starts eating. "My name really is Gabriel," he is telling me. "Gabriel Salvatore. You can look at my driver's license."

Now when I get to a phone I can tell the cops his name. Excellent.

"Good kitty," he says absently, petting the cat. His gesture is so gentle it totally confuses me.

"Did you come into my bedroom when I was four?" I ask.

His dark eyes sparkle. "You remember that?"

I start shaking again. "You said you were my guardian angel even then."

"I said something like that. You misunderstood me."

"Why?" My voice rises to a wail. "Why would you track me all my life?"

"What I told you that night was that I was trying to become your legal guardian. So your mother couldn't ditch you into foster care like she wanted to."

The cat finishes the stew and jumps into the tub to play with the drip. The music pounds my brain. I already know everything he is about to tell me. My bones know.

"I let you down, Hunter. I couldn't get custody because of all the mistakes I'd made. And then, I really was going to follow you all your life and watch out for you, but something else happened and I couldn't get to you until now."

I want to ask him all kinds of questions to keep him from telling me the central fact that is slowly invading my brain like a spreading stain. "You've been in jail, haven't you?"

He lowers his head.

"What for?"

"Your mother. How could she give up a great little boy like you? You were a terrific little boy, Hunter. I got mad at her. I got so mad when I found out she'd signed you away to the state."

"Mad like just now when you got mad at Stephanie." That explains the long prison sentence. I wonder why on earth they didn't make it longer. I feel like crying for someone, but I don't know if it's me or Stephanie or maybe my real mother, who I can't even remember. And now I'll never see her.

"The song is from Beethoven," he says. "It was adapted with these lyrics by some Italian guy. I don't know anything about music, but when I was . . . in prison, my roommate was a genius. He knew a lot about music. He gave me this song like a gift. I listened to it again and again, so I would never forget my mission. To find you when I got out."

I'm too tired to fight it, the fact that's coming at me like a giant meteor.

"It's called 'Lost Son.' It's about a father whose son is captured by the elf king. The father is too late and can't save his son. 'Figlio Perduto.'"

I'm silent. My head is down. The music swirls around me like a drowning pool.

"We have to get out of Fort Lauderdale, Hunter. They'll be coming for me. They'll be looking for you."

I begin to cry. It starts slowly and then it heaves and flows, like when you're really sick and puking your guts out. I don't know if I'm crying because I think they will never come looking for me and my father. Or because I think they will.

Chapter 11

"Figlio Perduto" plays on an endless loop. It appears to be Gabriel Salvatore's own custom-burned CD—eleven tracks of "Figlio Perduto." The last track always cuts off at "Papa, oh, Papa!" before cycling back to the beginning. *Papa, oh, Papa, please turn that thing off!*

We left Fort Lauderdale around six this morning. I was sleepy and it seemed unreal, being marched out to the van in total silence, like some guy in a prison movie. When I get into the van I see he's bought coffee and a dozen doughnuts, and, even more disorienting, he's brought along the cat, who is stretched out on the floor in the back. But just when I think I'm really in an episode of *The Brady Bunch* entitled "Goes on the Road," I notice he's removed the door handle on my side.

It's noon now and we're going north on I-95. No sign of those Amber Alert notices that are supposed to save the day for kids like me. I wonder if anyone's even found Stephanie yet. If she's dead. If she's not dead, she'd report me missing, wouldn't she? Wouldn't she?

We're passing through the exit signs for Daytona Beach now.

"Come on, Hunter," he says. "You must have to go to the bathroom now."

True. In fact, I'm about to explode. I look over at him. I notice he didn't shave this morning. I wonder if he's growing a beard to hide his identity. "Will you let me go by myself?"

He looks at me. His eyes look a lot like mine. "Eventually, of course, but right now I don't trust you. We just don't know each other."

"All the more reason to not go to the bathroom together!" I blurt. Okay, I'm a shy guy. Sue me.

He chuckles. "You'd never make it in prison."

"Well, up till now that wasn't in my career plans anyway." *Jeez, I'm talking and I can't shut up.*

But again, he just laughs. "It's never in anybody's plans, Hunter."

He cuts off the engine, stopping the hideous song. "Okay, tell you what. You can start earning my trust right now." He takes out his wallet. "Go to the bathroom and buy us some lunch. I can see everything from here.

If you do all that nicely, maybe we can loosen up the rules. Is that fair?"

"That's totally fair," I say, trying to think fast. "Thank you."

"But I'm watching. If I see you saying something to the lady in there or acting weird or anything, then we're gonna have to do this whole thing differently. Okay?"

Differently. Hog-tied and drugged? Beaten senseless? I really don't want to know. "Thanks." I take his money and wait for him to open my door.

Shaking, I push open the heavy glass door. Bathroom door, visible from van, straight back, lady at the counter, paying no attention to me, to my right. I'm looking, as I walk the preciously short distance, for something to write with. Lots of food here, but no office supplies. I don't even see lipstick or anything. I go on into the restroom, defeated.

But while I'm in there, I think, the counter lady has to have a pen because people are using charge cards. Can I write a note on my money right in front of her? How long could I take before he'd see what I was doing?

I look at the walls around me, all the information about who loves whom and who sux, and think if just one of those guys had left his pen or marker behind, I'd have some hope.

On the way out of the bathroom, I see the pens. They

were at the end of the rack, where I couldn't see them on my way in. I snag one without even thinking. Guess Dad is right, how easy it is to become a criminal. I walk around the back of a rack, pretending to look at potato chips, my heart working like a jackhammer, rip the pen out of its paper backing (harder than it should be), and scribble on my money, *Help FL#006HVN*. Even though my body is in a total panic, I have a strange sense of calm and precision as I pick up fruit, wrapped sandwiches, and chips. I glance outside and see my father watching me attentively and not looking at all disturbed.

The woman behind the counter smiles at me. She has the vague expression of a complete idiot, but I refuse to be discouraged. I slide my bill to her and say, "Here's my money!" Surely that will sound weird to her but not look weird through glass.

She picks it up and it slides into the cash register drawer. She starts counting out change. *Oh, come on!*

"Hey," I say, "did I give you a ten or a twenty?"

"Huh?" The drawer is open, my cry for help staring up at her.

"The *bill* I gave you. Was that a ten or a twenty?"

She doesn't look. "It was a twenty." She counts out the change. I walk back to my jailer with my sack of groceries. Still, my note is out there somewhere. Maybe somebody will see it eventually.

I can open the door from the outside.

"What'd you get?" he asks. "I'm starved."

"I don't know." I really can't hide my disappointment.

He paws through it, picks some meat out of a sandwich, and feeds it to the cat. "Thanks, Hunter. I'm really proud of you."

"What?"

"I watched you. You didn't say anything to her. It was a test. I . . . Hunter, I know I'm taking you against your will and everything, but I know once we've been together awhile, it won't be like that. Once you give me a chance. You weren't happy in that other home. I'm your father. Isn't this really the best place for you to be?"

"I don't know," I say honestly as he starts up the car.

"Okay," he says. "Okay, that's a start. I don't expect you to feel comfortable with me right away. But I . . . I picture . . . eventually we'll be like a real father and son. Shouldn't we have a chance to do that?"

Part of me wants to agree with him. "I don't know."

"If there's something I can do, like just now, showing some trust in you. If there's something I can do to make this easier for you, tell me."

Now I feel sort of bad about the note. No, I don't. Yes, I do. This whole thing is making me mad.

"Well, for one thing, you could turn off that CD! It's driving me out of my mind!"

I think to myself, now I'm going to get it. But he just looks sort of hurt for a minute and then kind of smiles. "Okay," he says. "I don't need it anyway. You're not lost anymore." He pulls it out of the slot and rolls down his window. "Fresh start." He pushes the radio button and Pitbull comes on with "Secret Admirer." Much better.

He smiles at me. I find myself smiling back. "Anything else?" he asks.

I unwrap my sandwich. "What's your cat's name?"

He's looking at the highway now and his smile gets bigger. "Cowboy. And he's our cat."

"And where are we going?"

"I don't know yet. We're looking for a place to make a home."

I keep quiet for a long time after that. Partly because I want to cry and partly because I'm having this huge argument with myself. If someone wants to finally give me a home after thirteen years, why would I want to get away from them?

⬧

We turn west on Route 10 and get as far as Winfield, Florida, before we're both worn out and tired of having the sun in our eyes. We find a Holiday Inn and have burgers and fries and take the leftovers back to our room, where I feed some of them to Cowboy, while my new father fiddles with the TV.

"You have a favorite show?" he asks.

I keep catching myself staring at him. He's really tall and I wonder if I have a shot at turning out that way— some guys have a big growth spurt in high school, I've heard. He moves like me, in some kind of way I can't even put into words. I know before he does it what he'll do with his hands, where his eyes will look next.

"It's Monday night," I say, climbing up onto the bed. "*RAW* is on."

He turns around, confused, like he thinks it's a porn show, and then says, "Oh! Wrestling! That's right, you like that stuff, don't you?"

You should know. You used Rolan Thunder's poster to hide your microphone. "Yeah. I used to watch it with my foster father."

"Mike," he says. He's always eager to show me he knows stuff about me. At this moment it's more flattering than creepy.

"Yeah. We had all these females in the house and Mike and I, you know, when we needed to just have guy time, we learned that if you turn on wrestling, the women tend to clear the room."

He laughs, looking at the screen where Johnny Come

Lately is walking up and down the ring with a microphone. The crowd is booing so loud you can hardly hear what he's saying. My father settles on the bed next to me. He peers at the screen like there's going to be a quiz on this material. "That's Rolan Thunder there, right?" he says hopefully.

"No," I say. "This is a jerk."

Cowboy jumps on the bed and curls up between us. I try not to hear *The Brady Bunch* song in my head.

"What do you like about Rolan Thunder?" Dad asks.

I wish he'd stop this kind of stuff because it's touching. And I think it's hypnotizing me, keeping me from realizing this situation can't work and I should be making a run for it as we speak. "Well, he's got this sort of I-don't-care persona. Like everyone else is so intense and yelling and growling and he's all mellow . . . but then he gets in the ring and he's all action and speed and kicking guys in the jaw. . . ."

He stuffs some cold fries into his mouth. "That sounds like me," he says, almost to himself.

I decide not to answer that. We watch for a while and it's clear he likes it. He laughs in all the right places. He definitely likes when the divas come out. I notice something weird, looking at his hands. They look exactly like mine. The shape of the fingers, the shape of the nails, even the way his hand is positioned, resting on his knee, it's the image of my hand. I've never known this. In all my life, never known anyone who was related to me. I think this is something regular kids take for granted because it's just there in front of them, but it's like . . . until you know there's someone on Earth who's like you . . . you're never sure you're okay as a person.

By the time we get to the main event, he's asleep with his arm across his eyes. The door is right there. But I don't use it.

Chapter 12

We drive through Tallahassee, Mobile, Lafayette, Houston. From hammocks to wetlands to oil derricks. When we cross the Colorado River, I feel something break loose inside me. I think it's my connection to Florida and the past. It feels great to cross a river and forget all those homes and families that didn't want me. I realize I don't even care if Stephanie is alive or dead. The only tie I can't seem to break is with Jessie. I think about her all the time, for some crazy reason.

Just outside Phoenix, we sell the van, motorcycle, and surveillance equipment. He buys a used Malibu for nine hundred dollars and pockets the profits. Now if anyone's looking for Florida plates, we won't have them.

"Are we running out of money?" I shout over the wind. The AC in the Malibu doesn't work so good.

"I have money," he says. In Lafayette, he cut his hair off and dyed it a sandy brown color. So now he looks a lot more like me. He looks nothing like an angel at this point, in his slept-in shirt and scruffy little beard. When I'm allowed to talk to people, he has me give my name as Salvatore instead of LaSalle, the name they gave me in the orphanage. I think it's a little weird he's disguising himself and using his real name, but I guess if he was good at being a criminal he never would have gone to prison.

"What do you do?" I'm amazed I hadn't thought to ask that before.

"I'm a landscaper," he says. His hands shift on the wheel, thumbs turning up. His whole body relaxes when he thinks about it. "I had my own company for a year. I'm really good at it. The customers like me, I love the outdoors, and I'm very particular about—what's wrong, Hunter? Why are you crying?"

I'm slumped, head between my knees, heaving out sobs. "Damn you!" I choke out. "You really are my father!"

❧

We sit on huge sandstone boulders in the middle of the desert, eating sandwiches wrapped in waxed paper, drinking the runoff from a bag of ice we bought a few miles back. Cowboy dozes in the sun nearby. I still think about making a run for it, but the feeling is kind of fading. For one thing, I feel like I need to ask some things and I feel like the time is now.

"Tell me about my mother," I say.

He looks up, guilty and startled. "Huh?"

The desert has put me in a weird mood. I'm so far from home now and Arizona looks like another planet. There's nothing but miles of red dirt and red rocks with little clumps of sagebrush and some kind of menacing mountains off in the distance. The sky above us is like a flat blue ceiling. I feel reckless here, like you do in a dream, when on some level, you know nothing you do really matters.

"Hunter, look. What happened to your mother was an accident. I paid for . . ."

"Yeah, yeah, yeah," I say, hefting up the ice bag and sucking water through the hole he punched in it. He has good survival ideas and instincts. "I'm not interested in that," I lie. "I want to know what my mother was like."

Something about the angle of the sun has given us long black shadows that cross. He starts slapping his pockets, looking for cigarettes that aren't there. "What do you want to know?"

"What was her name?"

His body actually flinches, like I hit him. "Oh, jeez, Hunter. You don't know her name?"

I hold his eyes. "How would I?"

"Oh, Christ. Courtney. Her name was Courtney. Courtney Driscoll." He pauses, and looks down. "When I say her full name like that, it takes me back to the trial."

No, this is MY therapy session. The wind is blowing in rhythmic gusts, and I tip my head back to let it cool my face. "What was she like?"

"Like?"

"What did she look like? Did she look like me?" The wind gets into my eyes and makes them tear up.

He scans my face. "Her hair was the same color as yours. And she was short, you know, built like you—uh—"

"Scrawny?"

"You're not scrawny! You just don't have a big frame."

"Was she smart?"

"Smart?"

"Smart! Why are you repeating all the questions like that?"

He takes a big bite of sandwich. "They just seem like weird questions! And they make me feel bad. I loved her at one time and I . . . hurt her. I don't want to think about it."

"Do you know everything about *your* father and mother?"

"Well, of course. I grew up with—"

"I grew up with nothing! No name, no family, no mother, no cousins, no family photo album, no Thanksgiving turkey, no—"

"Stop!" He actually puts his hands over his ears. "Jeez!"

I keep hammering. I'm not scared of him at all right now. "You're doing all this because you want to make it up to me. Right? Well, this is where you start. Whatever pieces of my jigsaw puzzle you've got, I want them. Right now."

He looks at me like I scare him. The wind tosses his hair around. When he speaks again his voice is very low. "I met Courtney in high school."

"Which one?"

"Piper. I was a junior and she was a freshman. She wore glasses. She sang in the chorus. Frankly, she was one of those girls you'd never notice. You know what I mean? Neat, clean, quiet. Boring. Ran with a pack of losers—a fat girl, a girl who was legally blind, you know what I'm saying."

"She was a nerd. Was she smart?"

"Very. Got all A's and stuff. Honors this and honors that. Always holding a book up to her chest like a shield."

"And you? What kind of a kid were you?"

"Would-be biker. I already had my first bike, a little Harley 883—"

"When you were just a junior in high school? How'd you afford that?"

"I don't know." His eyes shift away. "Anyway, I thought I was hot stuff. Wore leather, slouched in doorways, gave everyone attitude. I probably looked like a big jerk. I hardly came to school, drank beer, smoked pot, broke hearts—that kind of thing."

We laugh together. "So how did someone like you hook up with someone like her? You needed her for your heartbreaking quota? You had a bet with your friends?"

"Who said I had friends? No, here's the weird thing, Hunter. She came after me. One day I was just hanging around my locker and she gave me a plate of brownies she'd made in home ec."

My heart aches for Courtney Driscoll, bringing her brownies to the school bad boy. I think about Carolina, how crazy I was about her for a while there. "So you took advantage of her, right?"

"No! Not right away! I guess I thought she was out of her mind. I hardly even thought of Courtney as a girl. My idea of a girl was something with blond hair, black roots, and busting out of a tube top. But Courtney was on a mission to make me notice her. A couple days later she asked me for a ride on the bike."

"And?" Even though this makes me uncomfortable, I pretend it doesn't so I'll hear everything.

"She didn't hold me by the waist. She put her hands down on my legs. Well, I'm slow, but I'm not that slow."

"So *then* you took advantage of her?"

"Sure. I'm a human being, after all. The next day in school, her shield was dropped and she had on a sweater instead of the stiff shirts she'd been wearing. She had—a good figure. I started thinking she was really pretty."

"Don't go into a bunch of details about the sex."

"I wasn't going to." He laughs. "Anyway, we had a couple of dates and both our parents went crazy. Her father thought I was a hood."

"A what?"

"A bad guy. A ne'er-do-well. Like a gangbanger now."

"Oh, okay."

"But that, like, sealed the deal for both of us. We had a good thing going, which you don't want to hear about, and we were making our parents mad at the same time. Teenager heaven."

"Why would your parents object to her?"

"Huh?" The eyes slide away again.

"She was a nice girl, a good student. Why would they object to her?"

"Uh, I don't know. It's getting hot. Let's talk some more while we drive. We should be getting—"

"I want to know!"

"I don't know, Hunter. Maybe because she was Protestant and they were Catholic. I really don't know."

"Yes, you do. What was wrong with her? What are you keeping from me?"

"Nothing! You know how parents are. They thought she was after . . . I really don't know."

I think back to the last detail that didn't make sense. Him having a motorcycle as soon as he was old enough. "Your parents had money!" I shout like an accusation.

"No!" he says, like it is one. "I mean they weren't exactly poor. . . ."

"You were some kind of little rich kid acting tough with your leather and your bike! Weren't you? My mom was just middle class and your parents had a fit."

Busted, he leans back on his elbows and considers the big blue sky. "Jeez, Hunter, it's like you were there."

We sit for a while, in the rhythmic wind. I'm not done, but I want to let him rest. He reaches over and scratches Cowboy behind the ears. Cowboy shakes his head violently and resumes his nap.

"And then she got pregnant," I say after a while.

"Hunter, I'm hot. Let's at least drive and talk."

"No, I'm afraid you'll stop. This stuff is very important to me."

He sighs like a child. "Then she got pregnant."

I can hardly breathe. This is like I'm standing in the doorway of the bank vault and no alarm is ringing. I can take what I want.

"I was seventeen, Hunter. I didn't want to marry your mother. But—abortion, forget it. I couldn't stand that idea. Even then—you were my child. I couldn't give away my child. I don't know how other people do it. I thought my parents would help me raise you."

I miss some of this because I want to figure his age. He's only thirty. "Your family? What about her family?"

"They wanted Courtney to put you up for adoption." His eyes have gotten shifty and careful again. The wind picks up suddenly and blows hard and steady.

"What did Courtney want?" I lean forward to make him look me in the eye.

"She wanted to do that too. Put you up for adoption. I was the only one who—"

"But I ended up with her, right? I was with her the night you came into my room. Right before she did adopt me out. But for my first four years I was with her."

139

"It was all a big legal mess, Hunter. I don't understand half of it. After you were born, at the hospital, there were papers about giving you up for adoption. I said I wouldn't do it. Everybody thought I'd cave but I didn't. So I had the right, somehow, to block Courtney, but that didn't mean I could be the custodial parent because of some other stuff I had."

"What stuff?"

"I'd been arrested a couple of times. Bad boy, remember?"

"So you had the power to force her to keep me? Is that what you're saying?"

"That's how it worked out. I still don't totally understand. I was the one who wanted you—but then her parents jumped in and said they'd take you before they'd let my parents take you—the court ruled and you went to them. I had to take a blood test and go to another court just to visit you, which they still made it really hard to do. But I paid child support and everything. I was trying to keep my rights. And I figured if I worked hard and didn't have any more arrests—"

"What were you arrested for?"

"Just baby junk. Shoplifting. Possession. I don't know."

Nothing like later, when it was murder. "And you were trying to get the custody eventually."

"But I couldn't and then somehow when you were four, she tried to live on her own and she screwed up and then they told her she should give you up. Nobody would help me, my parents, her parents. I wanted you, but nobody would help me."

I give him a minute. He needs a minute. He collects all our lunch trash and folds it up, creasing the waxed paper. He pours the rest of the melted ice on the ground. I've noticed in our travels, he never litters.

"Will you tell me the rest?" I ask in a low voice. "Will you tell me how she died?"

He looks at me a long time, making his decision. I know he'll decide to trust me. What I don't expect is the way his eyes now fill up with tears, like when you dig a hole in the beach and water seeps in from underneath. He brushes them off but more come back. "I decided the thing to do was marry her. I thought she would do it and then I knew I'd have some real legal control. And maybe as a couple we'd have a stronger position legally. That's when I went to see you. I told you I was going to marry your mother and that I'd be able to watch over you all your life."

Now my eyes fill up because that's the phrase I

remember. "And that's where you said 'guardian' to me and I got the whole angel idea."

"Right."

"And later you exploited that." I need to say this even though he's crying.

"I did."

"So what happened with my mother?"

"She wasn't buying what I was selling. I begged her, if she wouldn't marry me to just give you to me . . . anything so you wouldn't get . . ."

"Lost."

"Yes!"

"And?"

"She had changed, Hunter. She was so angry at me. I cost her everything. College, her future. All because of what I did in the hospital. She hated me. She said the best way to get revenge was to make sure I never got my hands on you again and that she was damn well going to dump you into the system. She was, like, laughing at my feelings for you. Like it was something stupid. Like . . ." He coughs.

"Right."

The cough turns into a sob. I keep waiting, because I want to hear the end. I have a right to hear the end. "I lost control. I was so mad. She was, like, taunting me and I lost control. . . ."

"Okay. That's enough." I touch him, to break the spell. I know the rest anyway. I saw what he did to Stephanie.

His head hangs low. Tears darken the sandstone in little spots, like raindrops. "Is it wrong to want to keep people from hurting my own kid? When I got out . . . and I saw the home you were in. That bitch Stephanie . . . I wasn't going to interfere as long as the guy was there. But when he died . . . I didn't know if that woman would be good to you. I had to know. . . . I'm not evil, Hunter. I'm not. I'm not an angel or a devil. I'm just a man."

Our shadows have uncrossed. The wind has turned cold. The temperature changes fast in the desert. Cowboy gets up and stretches. I touch my father's arm. "It's time to go."

We drive through Quartzsite and Blythe, past the Salton Sea and the Joshua Tree National Park. Since I'm the one holding the map, I notice we're starting to run out of land.

"What are you going to do when we get to the ocean?" I ask. "Turn and go back the other way?"

He laughs. "Nope. I've decided we're going to Los Angeles. I've always wanted to live there. Isn't that cool? It's a big city, we can disappear, everyone needs landscaping work. It's perfect."

I glance up and see the exit sign for San Bernardino. Then it hits me and I start to laugh.

"What?" He almost swerves, trying to look at me. "What?"

"Los Angeles," I giggle, beside myself. I think I might be hysterical. "You're taking me to the city of angels!"

Chapter 13

"**Hunter! Come on,** man. Your breakfast is getting cold."

I'm almost ready. Just choosing between my new Skechers and my new Lugz. I go with the Skechers.

We have a little eat-in breakfast area in our apartment in Glendale. Dad's already in his coveralls, standing over the table, staring at my scrambled eggs to keep them warm. He cooks breakfast, I cook dinner.

I sit down and savor the smell. Dad's a good cook, puts things like Parmesan cheese in the eggs. The toast is buttered perfectly, like for a photo shoot. A multivitamin lies next to my orange juice.

He starts piling dishes in the sink. "I might be late tonight—we've got that Brentwood development today."

I laugh. He tells good stories about the fussy housekeepers in the Brentwood development and all their special instructions.

"What are you going to do?" He runs a sinkful of suds, his back to me. House arrest is technically over—after all, he can't take me to work with him or lock me in the apartment. But he asks me what I'm doing every day and certain things are off-limits. I can't talk to anyone, can't go to the library or a cybercafe (e-mail access), have to avoid police stations, and things like that. Some of this bothers me a little, but so far I play by his rules. I'm happy here. Plus, he's really good at spying.

"It's time to go to the Laundromat again," I say. "Want anything from the store?"

He flips around, opening the fridge, takes an inventory. "Nope. Looks well-stocked to me. Unless you need anything special for dinner."

I'm gobbling eggs. They are soooo good. "I might get some sour cream. I was thinking of beef Stroganoff." Jessie's recipe. That part of my life is like a dream now.

"Oh, wow. That sounds good. Except, remember I could be late. Don't make something that won't hold." He's going through his pocket-slapping routine now, ready for takeoff. Keys, ID badge, wallet. "Oh, I almost forgot. I got you a present yesterday."

I get a lot of presents these days but I still get pretty excited. "What?"

His fishes in his wallet and takes out two tickets.

"Oh, my God!" I scream. "The WWE?"

He grins. "Read 'em and weep."

It's not just a house show. It's not even a TV taping. It's the upcoming pay-per-view—Destruction, at the Staples Center. They've been advertising it all over town. In fact, I had already made plans to hang out there the afternoon of, because sometimes you can see the wrestlers arriving, rental cars for the undercard and big stretch limos for the main eventers. Sometimes they wave, out of charity. That's all I expected. But now I stare at these tickets and see I'm gonna be ringside. "Dad . . ." I read the ticket over several times and hold it to my heart. "This is, this is . . ."

"Big?" He grins.

"Huge." I pass them back reverently.

"Good. I was going for huge." He's still smiling as he walks out the door.

I sit and savor my eggs in our sunny, quiet apartment. Outside the sliding door there's a sycamore tree. It's beautiful. California is beautiful.

I turn on the radio and hum while I go around the apartment, collecting laundry and making a short list of Stroganoff ingredients.

It's like Dad and I are playing house, acting out

scenes from a sitcom. Well, that's what we have to do. That's the only place either of us has ever seen what a happy family is supposed to look like.

<hr/>

Glendale is cool. A huge mall, really good restaurants, and lots of kids. They bother me today. It's Saturday and they're out skateboarding and riding bikes. They all have someone to talk to. I'm hoping eventually Dad will let me enroll in school, but right now he says that's out of the question. He doesn't want any contact with any system anywhere. But I worry I'm going to fall behind and get stupid, or be even more socially warped than I was before. If I went to school, it would be Theodore Roosevelt Middle. I know where it is. I walk by there sometimes, since he hasn't put that off-limits. I wonder which kids might be my friends. No one probably. I'm better off just being grateful for what I have. I never thought I'd ever have a real parent like this. So what if there are some crazy temporary rules?

So why, on this near-perfect day, do I find my feet heading toward Harvard Street? To the library? Well, I tell myself, I should read some books so I won't get too stupid. Of course Dad would take me to Barnes & Noble and buy me anything I wanted. Okay, I'll admit it. I want to know if my old e-mail account is still there. If anyone is looking for me.

As I walk deeper and deeper into the forbidden zone, I wonder what Dad would actually do if he found out I went someplace I wasn't supposed to. I'm only two blocks from the library now, moving like I'm in some kind of trance. He's at work in Brentwood. He's not omniscient. He'll never know where I went today.

I stand across the street from the library. I watch a few people go in and out. I think about when I lived in the orphanage and they told us the story of Adam and Eve. I was always so pissed off at them. Why would you risk paradise just to eat a forbidden apple? But today, I get it—they just had to know.

I cross the street.

<hr />

From: hestia13@yahoo.com
To: shoehorn6@yahoo.com
Hunter—I say a prayer for you every day. I will never forget you. I wrote a letter to America's Most Wanted but I have not heard back. We are both very happy in our new home. We still talk to Stephanie and she says the police say they will find you. I hope so. Your friend, Jessie.

My heart pounds. Just seeing her name messes me up, reverses everything. Now that world seems like reality and my life here in Los Angeles seems like a dream. I have two other messages from her, sent earlier. With e-mail, you're always looking backward through time. I already have one extremely important piece of information. Stephanie's not dead. I can also infer that Jessie and one of my other sisters are together in a new foster home. I need a little pause, so instead of dropping down to the next e-mail from Jessie, I hit delete and drop to the next one in line, some spam from Amazon.com.

Dear Hunter—

We have new books for heart, mind, and body!
Check out *Angels, Protectors, and Spirit Guides* by Ariel Powers. If you order $25 dollars or more, your shipping is free!

This does nothing to slow down my heart rate. I've never ordered any books from Amazon in my life, much less angel books. I always did my research in the school library. Is this a sign or just a really, really big coincidence? If my father isn't playing head games with me anymore, who is? I hit delete fast.

The next one is from Jessie again, two weeks earlier.

Hunter—

The police told us that even if you were kidnapped, you might find an opportunity to check your e-mail. Hunter, if you ran away and you don't want anyone to find you, just answer this and tell me you're okay. I worry about you all the time. Your story is all over the news but I'm afraid that the attention will die down and people will stop looking for you and assume you're dead. Hunter, even if you can't answer this, I want you to know that you were my best friend in this world and I even had kind of a crush on you, but I guess you knew that. I pray for you and hope you're okay.

I'm slamming that delete key like it's an enemy. The next e-mail is from Andrea!

Hi, Hunter—
The sheriff's office says we should e-mail you in case you have run away, to tell you to please contact us so we can all have closure. Or if you know anything about the man who attacked Stephanie. I know we've had our problems, but I really hope you're okay. Answer if you can. Your sister, Andrea

I tremble as I hit delete, feeling the weight of all these people and their concern. My next e-mail is from Drew, obviously also sheriff-inspired.

Dear Hunter
Hi Hunter. Are you okay? Did you run away from home? Please come back. I got adopted and I have a

cat named Picky. You can pet her if you want. Only if you come back. I love you. You are still my best brother. XOXOXOXOXO Drew.

My delete hand freezes. I watch the cursor blink over Drew's X's and O's. I put my head down to stop from passing out. I feel the same way I felt when I had my tonsils out at six, coming out of anesthesia. My last e-mail—actually my first—is from Jessie again.

Hunter—

I hope you get this message. Everything has been so scary and I'm so scared for you. The whole thing was on the news. Stephanie says a man broke in and tried to kill her. When the social worker got there she was on the floor unconscious and you were gone. They say they don't know if you were abducted, or if you ran away with the man who attacked her, or if you just ran away period. I can't sleep at nights, thinking that a bad man has you and is hurting you. If you can answer this, please, please tell me you're okay. I'll keep any secrets you want, but I don't want to go forever not knowing how you are. The publicity has helped us all. There's a family that wants to adopt Drew and another one that will take me and Andrea on "lease purchase"— you know the drill—but maybe we'll finally have a real home. Stephanie is kind of messed up but I think she will be okay. She's all alone now. I think about you every day, Hunter, and say a prayer that you are safe and someday I'll see you again. Your friend, Jessie.

This time, because all my other chances are deleted, I hit reply. I watch the cursor flash. Can I tell her I'm safe but to keep my secret and leave me alone? Jessie's a good person, but she does blow the whistle when she thinks it's for your own good. I've learned that the hard way over and over.

Then I wonder if there's some way the police would know I'm checking these e-mails right now, and maybe trace them to this computer here? I really don't know how this stuff works. I don't want my dad to go back to jail and me to go back to that system I know all too well.

I never should have looked at these. It's pulling at me now, my old life. It's touching to me that my sisters (and I still do think of them like that) care about me. And even more, it's amazing to me that the sheriffs seem to care about me too. I always thought I was completely invisible to everyone.

The cursor is blinking away, like it's impatient with my indecision.

My father has done so much to make this happen.

This is my life now and I deserve it, after all I've been through. Dad's saving up his money. He's going to buy his own landscaping business someday and we'll be partners.

The damned cursor makes me want to scream. I see my father in Phoenix, unpacking our picnic. I see him throwing Stephanie against a wall. He manipulated me, spied on me. But he was desperate. He loves me. But he's also the guy who killed my mother.

I hit delete. Do you really want to delete this message? my server asks. I hit delete again.

I know what I have to do. But I have to do it by myself.

Hands shaking, I call up the *Sun Sentinel* Web site and input my own name. Six articles come up, dating from the day after I was kidnapped. I'm a celebrity. I choose the oldest article, figuring that will be the one with the most information. I realize there's something very specific that I'm looking for.

LOCAL BOY ABDUCTED
FOSTER MOTHER IN CRITICAL CONDITION

I'm really glad nobody thought I hurt Stephanie and ran away. I already know she's okay, so I scroll quickly through the story. Apparently Stephanie was able to tell them a man beat her up and snatched me. At the very end of the story, it says, *Police are looking into a possible connection with LaSalle's natural father, Gabriel Salvatore, who also disappeared around the same time. Police confirm that Salvatore is a person of interest and believe he may have vital information about the abduction.*

That's a nice way to put it. The story ends with a description of my dad's van and the license number. If all this weren't one day late, I think to myself, they might have caught us before we got out of Florida. But this article doesn't give me what I'm looking for. I go to the next one.

FATHER SOUGHT IN BOY'S DISAPPEARANCE

Police confirmed today that Gabriel Salvatore, 30, is now the primary suspect in the disappearance of Hunter LaSalle, 13, who was taken from his Coral Springs home Saturday after his foster mother, Stephanie O'Brien, was brutally assaulted. Salvatore was on probation for the murder of Courtney Driscoll, the boy's biological mother, nine years ago. The murder was apparently the result of a custody dispute. Sources close to the Broward Sheriff's Office tell us that surveillance equipment was found in Hunter's room and that the police are working on the theory that Salvatore stalked his son with the intention of kidnapping him.

I keep scrolling. I know I'm going to find what I want in this story. And there it is. A picture of this really scared-looking, mousy girl with the caption *Courtney Driscoll was murdered nine years ago.*

I'm looking at my mother. This is my mother. I see my own face and hair, my own cowardice, my own feelings of insignificance. She looks little, frail, temporary, like someone just waiting to be hit. Even though I've never known her, I know her. Even though she didn't want me, I know I'm her son.

I look at the picture of Stephanie in the same article, remember what he did to her, remember what he did to my mother. He's a fugitive. I'm a fugitive. Like my hope that I had a guardian angel . . . maybe this life I'm living is just another fantasy.

I shut off the computer, get up, and drag my dirty laundry home.

❧

"I thought we were going to have Stroganoff tonight," Dad says. He's been really quiet since he got home. I figured they gave him a hard time in Brentwood.

"You don't like this?" I made a stir-fry and I think it's pretty good.

He puts down his fork. "You didn't go to the store, did you, Hunter?"

I decide to keep eating, look calm. "Huh?"

"You didn't go to the Laundromat either. Because the hamper is full of dirty clothes." His voice is really quiet. Bad quiet.

I can't think what to do. I just keep shoveling food into my mouth. I wish it was this morning and I could do the day over. I was so happy when he gave me those tickets.

"So, where did you go?" he asks.

He knows. He totally knows. I don't know if I should keep evading or tell the truth. He's much harder to read than Stephanie ever was. I put my fork down. "I went to the library."

It's so quiet I hear Cowboy sneeze in the other room.

"But you're not supposed to go to the library, are you?"

I wonder if his voice got like this in his last conversation with my mother. Some people get really calm and quiet before they snap.

"Nooo . . ." I say. "But can't we change that rule? I just wanted to read a book. If I can't go to school, I should at least be able to—"

"You went to read your e-mail."

God! It's just like before when he was about a million steps ahead of me. "You don't know I did that."

"I check your account every day, Hunter. You've had some e-mails from your foster sisters for a while. Now they're deleted. You telling me you didn't do that?" He's talking in this super-reasonable voice, like an actor playing someone reasonable.

"How'd you get my password?"

"It was easy to guess. Thunder is your favorite wrestler. It was the first thing I tried."

The cat walks in and stares at us, like he can feel the tension in our conversation.

"You shouldn't do that." My voice sounds weak and scared.

"I should TRUST you?" he says. "Is that what I should do? Because if I had done that, you could have e-mailed the police and put my ass back in jail!" He doesn't sound so reasonable now.

I'm sweating. "But I wouldn't do that. I didn't. You must have looked at Sent Mail. I just read them and deleted them. Doesn't that count for something?"

He looks at me for the longest time. I wonder if he sees, like I do, that our eyes are identical. "Yes," he says. "It does count for something. But because you did this, Hunter, you just moved back a GIANT step."

He gets up suddenly, stands over me. I keep my head down. "A GIANT STEP!" I cringe. The cat runs out of the room. But he doesn't hit me. He catches himself. He walks back to his place at the table and sits down heavily.

"So for a while, until I start trusting you again, I think you better stay in during the day. We can run errands together on Sundays."

I notice that under the table, my legs are shaking. I need to make him happy. I need to get him calm. "I understand."

"And you really, really shouldn't think about defying me again like that. Because I'm smarter than you, Hunter. And you'll get caught every time. And the less trust I have, the less freedom you'll have."

I picture myself locked in the bathroom, like when he first captured me. He's capable of doing that. He's capable of a lot of things. I think about that old bumper sticker IF YOU LOVE SOMETHING, LET IT GO. THEN HUNT IT DOWN AND KILL IT. "I'm really sorry, Dad."

"We can have so much fun, Hunter, if you just play by the rules. Don't screw up a good thing for both of us." He leaves the table.

I stand up, wobbling, and clear the plates. I'm still thinking of the Garden of Eden. Once you get the knowledge, you have to leave. My father is a desperate criminal and I'm still a prisoner. And anytime I make him unhappy, I'm in as much danger as anyone else who has ever crossed him. Like Stephanie. Like Mom.

My mother's face from the article flashes in my head again. He beat her to death. I wonder if she loved him as much as I do.

Chapter 14

Dark clouds roll into L.A. as we drive to the Staples Center. Dad says it's the beginning of the rainy season—that's what the other landscapers told him—a bad time for business, because you have to keep postponing and rescheduling work and everything grows out of control and the customers get cranky.

I've been to a couple of WWE house shows—once in a while Mike would wage a huge battle with Stephanie and convince her that the ticket prices weren't outrageous and that I needed a guy activity so I could recover from the stream of chick flicks Stephanie and the girls were always renting. About twice, she gave in, forcing us to buy the fifteen-dollar nosebleed seats, which make the wrestlers look like a colony of fighting ants, but still, it was cool to sit with Mike and cheer and do all the chants and stuff. Mike and I learned the second time that if you go to the arena early you can see the wrestlers come in their rental cars and limos.

I want to do the same thing now with my real father—have the ultimate guy-bonding experience. I have a right to some kind of memory like that. It's the least the universe can give me. Because soon, I know, I'm going to have to make a run for it. No matter how great my life seems now, I know I'm a prisoner and I'm living with the guy who killed my mom and who can turn on me at the drop of a hat and make Stephanie look like Mother of the Year. I'm just not sure when and how I'm going to leave.

"How do you know where the wrestlers will drive in?" Dad asks as we park the car.

I look up at the arena. The Staples Center has a very impressive shape, like Noah's Ark jumping in midair, and on top there's—well, you could only call it a steeple.

"We just walk around the arena and see where there's a cluster of crazy fans," I explain. "There!"

Sure enough, twenty or so fans are hanging over a railing to our right. We walk up there and see a loading area with a huge truck idling. "That's where the ring is," I explain to Dad. WWE flunkies in their yellow shirts are milling around, talking on headphones and interacting with LAPD officers, who are driving in and out and all around. I wonder if they stick around for the show.

"Did you see anybody yet?" I ask a kid. Little kids are your best information sources at these things.

"We saw Juan de Libre!" he screeches. "That's his car right there!" He points to a silver Toyota.

"It's not his car, stupid!" says his buddy. "It's a rental car. They all have rental cars."

"You're the one who's stupid!" says the first kid. "He lives in San Diego! It could be his real car."

An older guy, probably the father of one of these kids, smiles at my dad. "You know anything about this stuff?" he asks.

Dad's been watching *RAW* for the past few weeks, but he has trouble keeping any of it straight. "All I know is, if this guy"—he points to me—"sees somebody named Rolan Thunder, he's going to get hysterical."

I grin at him. I'm trying to memorize every happy moment.

The fans here are a mixture of ages and races, more males than females, more kids than adults, but there's a couple of really old people too. They must have come to see Jack Shine or something. I think it's kind of cool that some people have never outgrown being wrestling fans. I hope I'm like that.

Suddenly, about thirty police cars pull in. "Somebody big is coming!" I shout out, and the littler kids whirl around. And it's then I get this crazy idea. What if I tried to run right now? Just run to the nearest cop car and tell them who I am. Police are everywhere, there are thousands of witnesses, so he really couldn't do anything, and most of all, I'd have the element of surprise. He'd never expect me to bolt at a time like this, which makes it the perfect time to bolt. Doesn't it?

Suddenly, there's a flash of lightning so bright it seems like it's all around us. Several of the people in the crowd, including me, scream involuntarily and then laugh. Then we scream again at the thunderclap.

"Should we go in?" Dad asks. "I think the doors are open now."

I panic, not sure what I want to do. "Wait. Let's see who this is."

I say this because of a huge, collective squeal from the other fans. This time it's not for lightning. It's for a white stretch limo that's pulling in, accompanied by two police cars. We all forget the weather and hang over the railing, trying to see who gets out. It's Rolan Thunder. Oh my God. He looks amazing in person. Even in street clothes, you can see he's almost seven feet tall.

"Rolan!" I scream at him, because suddenly it's the

most important thing in the world for him to acknowl-
edge me.

He peers up at me. Me! And then he gives me the
thumbs-up. It feels like a sign.

Tears fill my eyes and spill over.

"What's wrong?" My dad tries to look into my face.

I cough and sputter. "A bug flew in my mouth. Let's
go in."

"We'll get you some water." He tries to put his arm
around me.

I shrug him off. "Let's just go in."

I can't believe the seats we have. We're ringside, on the
floor, within chair-throwing distance of all the action.
We're also on the aisle, I note. I still don't know if I'm
going to do anything or not. I keep thinking about all
those police cars out there. I feel like I felt my first time
on the diving board, voices in my head yelling, *Do it!
Don't do it!* I look around to make sure I know where the
nearest exit is. I see Dad glance at the beer guy. "Go
ahead." I nudge him. "Have fun."

He smiles at me. Guilt stabs my stomach. "Maybe
just one," he says. "Get yourself a Coke or something."

"Okay." I look around at the filling arena, trying
to get so caught up in the excitement that I won't

worry about what comes next. But I can't help myself. I scan the program, looking for the right match, somewhere in the middle of the card, where Dad will be lulled by beer and camaraderie into a false sense of security.

I rehearse in my mind. Review where all the police cars were parked, mentally walk myself over there. I would calmly tell my story and they could check it out. They'd believe me, wouldn't they? I wonder how long it would take before Dad got suspicious and came looking for me.

The announcer climbs into the ring to mixed noises and starts telling us all the things we can't do—videotape the show, point lasers at the wrestlers. My heart starts to pound. It's showtime.

∙

By the second match, I've lost all thread of what's going on in the ring. All I can do is rehearse. Down the aisle, through the door, run to a cop car. Down the aisle, through the door, run to a cop car.

"This is so cool!" Dad says. His voice seems to come from far away.

"Yeah."

"I wonder if I could have another beer and be a safe driver," he says.

"Go ahead. We're here to have fun." Anything to slow his reaction time.

He gives me a little pat on the shoulder. "This is one of the best times I've ever had in my life, Hunter."

I turn my face away fast.

⟳

I hear the giggling sound that signals Susie Cute. I figure this is the match. Dad will be distracted by a bunch of women rolling around more than anything else.

"I have to go to the bathroom," I scream over the cheering and catcalling.

"Now?" He can't take his eyes off the ring, where she's waving her cowboy hat.

"I shouldn't have had the Coke. Anyway, I want to get back for Rolan's match."

He sips his second beer, which is almost gone. "Suit yourself."

I get up and start walking. My arms and legs feel funny, like I just got off a trampoline. I hit the exit doors and come out into the concourse, speeding just a little. A couple of security guys eye me and I think of offering myself up to them, but so many jokers come to wrestling, I know they'd take me for a smart aleck. I walk through the long expanse of arena to the escalator, knees getting weaker all the time.

Through the glass, I can see and hear the mother of all thunderstorms, flashing, crashing, and pouring water over every side of the arena. I wonder if that's a good thing or a bad thing.

I'm at the bottom of the escalator. I see the door. I don't see a policeman anywhere.

"Hunter!"

I whirl. He's at the top of the escalator, smarter than I thought, faster than I could have dreamed. And now he knows I've betrayed him and I'm trying to run. I run.

"Hey, kid!" yells a security guy as I sprint for the door. "Don't run on these floors."

"Stop him!" Dad yells. "That's my son!"

I hit the doors so hard shock waves bounce in my shoulders. I run into the rain and then stop like a fool, wondering what to do. *Should have planned better. Should have planned better.*

Since I don't have a plan, I just keep running. I circle the arena, toward that loading area, still hoping a cop will be sitting in a car somewhere. It's a bad choice. I come to a ledge that I have to jump from. I look behind me and see Dad and the security guard, allies, in pursuit.

I give my best imitation of Rolan Thunder and leap like a frog to the lower level of concrete. Wrestling has taught me to land on my feet with my knees bent to absorb the shock. Lightning flashes so bright it blinds me, followed by a cannon blast of thunder. My hair is wet and hanging in my eyes.

Dad and Security are at the rail, not willing to imitate my frog splash. "Circle around on him!" Dad commands. "You go that way, I'll go this way."

Doesn't it occur to that guard to wonder why a kid would be running from his dad? I can't worry about that. I take off. My sneakers slide on the wet pavement. I cannot fall. I cannot fall.

I turn a corner and smack right into the security guard. "Kid, listen . . ." he begins.

He tries to wrap his arms around me. I throw my arms up to break the hold and actually give him a very sloppy version of the Spinning Heel Kick. Mine probably didn't look good enough for cable TV, but it knocks him off his feet and I keep going in the same direction, since I know Dad lurks in the other direction.

Rain whips my face and runs into my eyes. It's hard to see which way I want to go. I remember that the last time someone defied my father, he murdered them. That gives me lots of energy. Okay, I think, I need to get away from this arena and find a police station or someone who'll help me. That means I either have to stop and wait for a light or dodge L.A. traffic. Death either way. I hear Dad's feet striking the pavement behind me. "Hunter!" His voice is a roar, like a wild animal.

With no time to make a choice, I just swerve and

keep on running, which means circling the arena again. The lightning flashes and my animal response is to freeze. Dammit. That cost me seconds. When the thunder comes I force myself to keep running. His footsteps sound closer. I have to have a dad who's in shape. I realize he has as much at stake as me. If I get to the authorities, he might go back to prison. Both of us have life-or-death adrenaline.

Water is running down my collar and my chest feels like a truck ran over it. I want to quit. Rain makes you want to quit. I feel like I can't win. The only advantages I have are rubber soles and youth. I decide maybe I can wear him out, so I turn sharply and run up the arena steps. It's grueling, but it has to be worse for him. At this point it's all I've got. Like a zebra running from a lion. He's got the ferocity. All I have is running stamina.

Lightning flashes again. I hardly flinch. Now my legs and my chest are complaining and so is my dad.

"You little bastard!" he puffs. "I trusted you! You fucker!"

I have a new mantra. *He'll kill me if he catches me. He'll kill me if he catches me.* I think now I'll go back into the arena and throw myself on the mercy of the crowd. I'm safer in there than alone out here.

That's when my ankle turns and I go down. I slide, I

bump, I lose six or seven steps before I can catch myself. On the steps above me I see the freaking candy wrapper that is going to mean my death.

His hands close on my ankles like a hot vise. Now his voice is low. "You're going to be so sorry—"

"Help me! Help me!" I scream. Where are the security guys now? His knee somehow drives into my midsection, flipping me on my back so he can clamp his hand over my mouth. The stone steps bruise my back. Now I see his eyes and know I am dead. This is the last thing my mom saw. I am going to die here in the rain. I arch my back and look upside down at the arena, at the steeple thing, where now I see there is a carving of an angel I didn't notice before, pointing its finger down to me.

His hands close on my throat. "You had to ruin everything," he hisses. I start seeing sparkly things above his head.

The lightning and thunder are simultaneous now, the storm is right over us. A fork of light tears the black sky in half. I look up and see it strike the angel on the roof, illuminating it in a way that makes it look alive. The angel's pointing finger seems to aim at my father and then fire, silver fire, pours from the finger. I know we're going to be struck by lightning and I buck wildly.

Something like the wind blows me or throws me

away from him as the silver fire pours down and explodes like a bomb, hitting the metal trash can beside us. My father freezes, and in that moment, I finally see a police car pulling up to the stadium and I run toward it. "Help me!" I scream. "I've been kidnapped! He's a murderer!"

Chapter 15

"The weirdest part"—Jessie drags hard on her straw, sucking up mint green sludge—"is that there would be a carving of an angel on the top of a public arena. What with all the church-and-state stuff."

"There is no angel on top of the Staples Center." I suck at my own sludge, the color of the harvest moon. We agreed to meet at this place we used to like, called Do Me A Flavor. It has a hundred flavors of milkshakes. I don't know if this is a date or not.

"Huh?" She looks up at me. She got new glasses or something. She looks cute.

"After the trial was over, I made the police drive me over there. I wanted to see for myself. No angel."

"What do you make of that?"

This is the part I'd prefer to keep private, but Jessie has the kind of eyes that pull secrets out of you. "I'm talking to a priest about it now. Father Ruiz helped me a lot when—"

"When your father was stalking you and pretending to be an angel. Have you forgotten all that stuff was a scam, Hunter?"

"Yeah, that stuff was, but some of the other stuff that happened to me . . . once I started praying . . . it felt good. I think there are some kind of angels or spirits or something . . . out there."

Jessie pushes our milkshake glasses out of the way and takes both my hands. It feels weird. "But, Hunter, be careful. You were so open to that stuff and look what happened. You were conned."

I don't want to take my hands away and I don't want to leave them there. I take one hand back as a compromise. "Jessie, there's only two ways to be. Open or closed. If you're open, lots of bad stuff can get to you. If you're closed . . . nothing gets in at all. I've made my choice."

She squeezes my hand and then pulls back, signaling a new topic. "What's it like, living with the Salvatores?"

I take a final slurp and signal the server. I'm wondering if Jessie will go to the movies with me. "They're about a thousand years old and about this high." I indicate a level two feet off the floor. "They look like a set of salt and pepper shakers. How they gave birth to a big guy like my father I'll never know."

"But what's it like living with them? Are they good to you?"

I understood her question the first time but I didn't know how to answer it. "They bicker a lot and he gives me a hard time about every little dime I want to spend and she cries if I don't take second helpings of everything she cooks. And they say crazy things to me."

"Like what?"

"Like when I said I was coming to see you today, she said, 'Be careful. Don't leave her with a big belly.'"

It even takes Jessie a minute to know what that means and then she turns red and laughs her head off. I guess I had mocked Nonna's voice a little too. "But . . ." she says when she's finally done giggling.

"You heard a but?"

"I did."

"But, they're my grandparents. They love me. Nonno told me he made terrible mistakes raising my dad and he feels like I'm a second chance to get it right."

"You're with family," she sums up, understanding as only a foster kid can understand.

"Yes. And you? Do you and Andrea like your new family?"

She shrugs.

"Oh," I say. I really want to give her a hug, but, well, not today. Not yet. "You want to see a movie?"

She looks hopeful but wary. "Really?"

"Yes, really! I asked you out, didn't I?"

"Yes, but did you ask me out like a brother? Or like a guy?"

"Like a guy who used to be your brother." I try a charming smile but she's just giving that stare again. "Like a friend for today, okay? And then . . . you know, we'll see."

Some kind of little smile tugs at her mouth. She's way smart. Someday I'll tell her how and why my feelings for her have changed. It's because now I know how precious every person who loves me is. But she's gotten all she's going to get this day in the way of touchy-feely. "Let's go see *Firepower*," I say. "I heard that it's good."

But she's already felt the power shift and is running with the ball. "Let's go see *Girlfriend, Girlfriend*."

"Oh, man! Not a chick flick!"

Her little smile is back. "It's got Halle Berry."

I shake my head in defeat. "You're really smart, Jess."

"I hope so."

After the movie I walk her home, and then I walk over to the cemetery to visit Mike's grave. I visit here a lot. It

176

means two things to me. This is where I said good-bye to Mike and also where I first saw my father. When I come here I always hear that song Dad played, "Figlio Perduto." He's probably playing it in his cell right now. I remember how he drove up here in a cloud of dust, looking like an angel. Father Ruiz says that if I want to I can write to him, or even visit him someday. I might, but not yet. I can't sort him out in my mind. I don't know which parts of him were real and which were just my wishes and prayers.

I decide I'm tired and wait for a bus to take me home. The wind blows hard. The song is still in my head. All my life I wondered what it would be like to have real parents. What it would feel like. I thought it would be like having guardian angels, magical people who took perfect care of you and never made mistakes. Now I know it's nothing like that. My mom was flawed, but I love her. My dad is flawed, but I love him too. Having real parents is like having a song. A song that repeats in your mind, forever.

Acknowledgments

First and foremost, thanks to Alex Flinn for refusing to let me give up on this project through its many permutations. Thanks to Alex Flinn, Heidi Boehringer, and Laurie Friedman for essential feedback on the manuscript. Thanks to Heidi Boehringer for information on motorcycles and to Kate Farrell and Marjetta Geerling for information on California. Thanks to George Nicholson for always embracing my crazy ideas. And as always, thanks to my husband, Jay, for being my guardian angel.